DIVERTIMENTO
·1889·

PUBLISHED WORKS BY GUIDO MORSELLI
(dates of composition in parenthesis)

Non-fiction

Proust, o del sentimento (1942–3) 1943
Realismo e fantasia: Dialoghi con Sereno (1943–7) 1947
Fede e critica (1955–6) 1977

Fiction

Incontro col comunista (1947–8) 1980
Un dramma borghese (1961–2) 1978
Il comunista (1964–5) 1976
Roma senza papa (1966–7) 1974
Contro-passato prossimo (1969–70) 1975
Divertimento 1889 (1970–71) 1975
Dissipatio H. G. (1972–3) 1977

DIVERTIMENTO
·1889·

GUIDO MORSELLI

———————— • ————————

Translated from the Italian
and with an Introduction by
Hugh Shankland

E. P. DUTTON   NEW YORK

Published in the United States by E. P. Dutton,
a division of NAL Penguin Inc.,
2 Park Avenue, New York, N.Y. 10016.

Originally published in Italy under the title
Divertimento 1889

Library of Congress Cataloging-in-Publication Data

Morselli, Guido.
Divertimento 1889.

Translation of: Divertimento 1889.
I. Title:
PQ4829.0714D513   1986   853′.914   86-32909
ISBN 0-525-24553-7

OBE

1 3 5 7 9 10 8 6 4 2

First American Edition

CONTENTS

——————— • ———————

INTRODUCTION

———————————— • ————————————

Italians, even some of Guido Morselli's closest friends, discovered only very recently that a formidably original novelist was lost when Morselli took his own life in 1973, at the age of sixty. Up till then not one of his novels had been accepted for publication – seven are now available in Italy – and all had been turned down by numerous publishers. How could such a major talent go unrecognised? The 'Morselli affair' compelled the literary establishment to ask itself some awkward questions. The easiest explanation for the rejection is that his work is unlike anything else in post-war Italian fiction.

But the rejection was to some extent mutual. 'They say that in solitude lies the only true happiness,' he wrote at thirty-five in *Realismo e fantasia* (Realism and Fantasy, 1947), an ambitious volume of philosophical dialogues, the second of the only two books he saw through the press, 'but in fact it is not so, indeed it is often no happiness at all. For some people solitude is a duty.' The little house he built for himself in a solitary mountain valley between Como and Lake Maggiore was the outward sign of this compulsion. With it went a deep love of the countryside, and a growing revulsion against modern life and its worst excesses, which in his last book he named Brutality, Pollution, Money-fever, and the wholesale Uglification of the world.

'Sometimes we would spend hours on end going over many things from the past,' a woman who was close to him recalls, 'old songs, old fashions, old trams, old trains (about which he knew everything), old streets, old houses that are gone. And yet he used to say he could happily have spent three months all alone on the moon.' In his bitter, self-confessional last novel, *Dissipatio H. G.* (The Dissolution of the Human Race), he insists it would not be right to call him a misanthrope, a hater of mankind; more accurate would be 'phobanthrope', one who lives in fear of the human race. An old game with him, he goes on, was to imagine the world as his alone, exclusively 'with me and for me', miraculously emptied of any other human presence. The poetic justice or divine punishment which he imagines for himself in that defiant, tragic book is a terrifying paradox: after deciding to drown himself in a mysterious subterranean Lake of Solitude because the presence of humanity has become too oppressive to live with, his body refuses at the crucial moment to execute the order and he returns to the world to discover that his day-dream has become an irreversible reality: the entire human race has 'passed away'. One of the revelations which he receives is that it is not the end of the world. 'What *were* they, what did they *do*?' the rest of nature asks after 'the great simplification'. 'They were neither necessary nor useful.' Maybe Morselli would have denied the infantile element in that deadly serious day-dream (he scorned Freud and childhood has no role in his fiction) but it shows what contradictory instincts within himself he had to fight against to achieve the adult courage, the fearless intelligence of his best work.

'Too many women, too much solitude, too many eccentricities,' is the way a Catholic critic rather censoriously summed up Morselli's life in an article that otherwise generously argued (against other theologians) that the writer's suicide was not incompatible with the religious spirit his work often reveals. He was born in 1912, the second of four children, and grew up in Milan, where his father was president of Italy's largest pharmaceutical company. His mother died when he was twelve. He missed her bitterly, but he also came to develop a profound admiration for his father, a strong-willed, hard-working man, and in the years after his father's death Morselli said he dreamt of him almost every night. Despite his cult of aloneness, Morselli's fiction is peopled with clear, positive-thinking men who stand out from their fellows for their unselfish honesty and realism.

It was largely to please his father that he read law at Milan University, but then, instead of settling down to a career, he travelled widely, including quite a long residence in England. Before being called up in 1940 on Italy's intervention in the war he had already tried his hand at some short stories and newspaper articles on current affairs, military history and railways. Until the last ten years of his life he continued to contribute occasional pieces to the cultural press on a wide variety of subjects, in particular history, philosophy, religion and literature. He was exceptionally fluent and well-read in the major European languages; in fact his non-conformism and an aversion to all rhetoric and excessive emotion gave him a spontaneously pan-European cast of thought, an anti-nationalism which in his fiction finds a geographical centre in the cultural diversity of old Austria, or in a lifelong love-hate relationship with polyglot, solid, neutral Switzerland.

Something of a manic depressive, his name for the human quality he most valued was *serenity*, 'the faculty of seeing the world as it really is'. In his philosophical writings it figures as a constructive balance between the polar opposites of 'fantasy' (subjectivity, introversion, idealism) and 'realism' (objectivity, participation, materialism). In his first published work, a lucid monograph on Proust's *A la recherche du temps perdu*, which he found time to write while he was a subaltern in Mussolini's army, he defined the consummate artist as 'a sensitive man with an exceptional fascination for ideas' and characteristically emphasised the outward-looking facets of Proust's intelligence: 'curiosity, clarity, versatility'.

Morselli experienced the carnage of war ('the most catastrophic and futile in history') in Southern Italy during the Italian débâcle of July–September 1943. When his unit was disbanded he remained marooned in Calabria for nearly three years, homesick and penniless, unable to get word to his family or to the woman he loved. In this intensely lonely period he began the extensive working journal which he kept for the rest of his life, drafted a first novel and the long philosophical dialogues, and at least at one point contemplated suicide. After the liberation of the north his father offered him a position in business, but Guido refused. 'The true artist,' he had already written in his *Proust*, 'impervious to taunts or cajolements shuts himself up in his ivory tower, since only in isolation can he be of value to his fellow man, labouring to offer him the incomparable gift of his work.'

That was the unashamedly romantic side of the man, and although he came to learn to treat it with irony and not a little suspicion he never abandoned the principle in either his thinking or his practice. For the rest of his life he lived (modestly) off the family fortune and his work was his writing. The experience of war and his long exile in Calabria left him with an extreme sensitivity to noise and a hatred of any form of travel, especially tourism. For twenty years he lived in his secluded valley beside a mountain called the Field of Flowers, surrounded by woods and wild animals, with distant views of Monte Rosa and the glaciers of the Bernese Oberland. Three months before he shot himself he had fled his home, following a desperate battle to block a planners' decision to construct a highway and maddened by the din of motor-cross enthusiasts who had popularised the valley.

After his early attempts at novel-writing in the 1940s, and a long interim of further journalism, plays, a film-script, two volumes of intense religious speculation and even a rigorous attempt to exorcise his demon in a 'Short Treatise on Suicide', he made a determined return to fiction in 1961. In *Un dramma borghese* (A Bourgeois Drama), a work of desolate realism, which seems to have been written in a fit of misogyny, the 'drama' is an eighteen-year-old daughter's passion for her widowed father. Rigidly schematic, it is a study of two unstable people tragically unmatched in intelligence (his) and emotion (hers). It is also a conscious challenge to prevailing orthodoxies of cultural politics in Italy, confronting its Oedipal theme with nothing but contempt for Freudian notions of the unconscious and presenting a resolutely uncommitted 'conservative' hero. In fact the real topic is Morselli's intriguingly ambiguous portrait of himself in the shape of an egocentric middle-aged neurotic fearfully defending his precariously constructed peace of mind from 'invasion' by others. Morselli admired altruism but he seems to have found it so rare that it never failed to astonish him. Shocking to the reader is not the father's sexual response to his daughter, but his incapacity to show a glimmer of affection for another human being in desperate need. Suicide, treated ironically, is a theme that runs through the book from beginning to end.

The title of his next novel, *Il comunista* (The Communist), does not indicate a political conversion, although one of Morselli's many serious intellectual interests was socialist thought and he was proud of his own 'evolutionary' version for which he coined the name 'socialidarity'. After having explored the negative side of his own ego so exhaustively he now suddenly reveals his astonishing versatility ('If they'd only publish me,' he used to say, 'I could treat a different subject every day.'), in particular a rare intuitive ability to evoke social or historical contexts remote from his own direct experience, and in a language which seems to speak faithfully for them. His working-class protagonist, an ex-railwayman and communist activist, is the first of his positive heroes, men whose talent lies in their creative approach to real life, a capacity to 'leave a mark on things and people'. *Il comunista* is also the tragic story of a man of sincere faith whose heresy is to assert, to the consternation of his party's official 'theologians', that no future society will ever eliminate the evil of work, understood as a biological fatality rather than an economic law, 'a state of continual tension'. In the mid-fifties Morselli had written a courageous volume of religious philosophy, *Fede e critica* (Faith and Criticism), largely concerned with the problem of evil, seen not as the devil's work but God's, and in its specific form of human pain and unhappiness, sickness and toil, conflict and war. Job is his hero, honoured for refusing to accept the orthodoxy that his intolerable misfortunes and sufferings could be his own fault or sin.

Veiled by many levels of grotesque irony, the same theme, 'the insoluble problem', also lies at the heart of *Roma senza papa* (Rome without the Pope), the most successful of his novels in Italy. Once again Morselli astonishes by the complete change of style and mood. Set in the year 1997 but written during the pontificate of Paul VI, the first globe-trotting pope, it is a wickedly inventive satire which makes a meal of the contradictions inherent in attempts to liberalise Roman Catholicism. Drugs are prescribed for instant mysticism, celibacy is eccentric, confessionals are computerised, euthanasia is okay and the GID (God Is Dead) movement is doing well among the seminarists. But Rome's greatest tourist asset, the Pope, has deserted the noisy circus of the eternal holiday city. His country retreat is not the luxury of Castelgandolfo but a little cluster of whitewashed buildings with green shutters in the middle of a field. When John XXIV, an Irishman and a keen tennis player whose life's work has been to demonstrate that everything has already been said, finally condescends to hold an audience, he laconically informs everyone that 'God is not a priest.'

Contro-passato prossimo (Past Conditional), completed in 1970, is Morselli's most ingenious work and his most optimistic, as though the failure of his hope in God had suddenly given him new faith in man. How it was never accepted for publication is beyond understanding, for it is an extraordinary feat of imagination and intelligence. With the materials of reality he conducts a cool experiment to challenge conventional notions of the historical process and demonstrate that nothing need necessarily happen as it does. Taking the whole context of European history as found in 1916 he proceeds vividly to chronicle a no less incredible sequel than the 'real' events: through just as plausible a combination of unfathomable accident and human design, a united Europe eventually emerges after victory goes to the Central Powers in time to prevent America's intervention in European affairs. Morselli's 'counter-history' celebrates the (impossible?) triumph of tolerance and reason over chauvinism and fanaticism and in great part it is achieved by the co-operative work of a small number of independent-thinking politicians and individuals, 'men of imagination and decision'.

The unnamed hero of *Divertimento 1889* is hardly notable for his imagination or decision. This man with one of the most 'loathsome and alienating' of jobs and a deep longing to escape from it, is united Italy's second monarch, King Umberto I, a rather less absolutist and certainly more conventional figure than his father, the national legend, Vittorio Emmanuele II. Like the old King he had little time for parliament and politicians, much more for military matters and mistresses: the Duchess Litta was already his official lover before his marriage to his beautiful cousin, Margherita, and remained so, not without rivals, until the end. Morselli's account of Umberto's character – the brisk military turn of mind and phrase, his philistinism, the moments of uncertainty and the lack of self-assurance, the streak of fatalism – all correspond to the historical record. In an obituary notice Reuter's man in Rome praised the 'simplicity of his habits' and 'the unostentatious way in which he performed his duties'. But for his own good reasons Morselli underplays the extent of the King's actual power, for in foreign and colonial policy and at certain moments of political and social tension Umberto I carried quite a lot of weight. Morselli, incidentally, knew the complications of keeping two or more women going at once. And one sees how a King who complains he has mountains of paperwork and no one who listens to him might earn the wry commiseration of a prolific unpublished novelist.

1889 did not bring too many unexpected headaches for His Royal Highness. The government under the volatile Sicilian, Francesco Crispi (fiercely anti-French champion of the 'Triple Alliance' between Germany, Austria and Italy), and his cool-headed Treasury Minister, the Piedmontese Giovanni Giolitti, had major bank scandals and a severe financial crisis to contend with. But in nineteenth-century Italy the monarchy was not too popular an institution in many quarters. The Papacy could not forgive the House of Savoy for seizing Rome, while Radicals, Socialists, and of course Republicans, were all nominally pledged to remove the King, and anarchist groups did not intend to work through parliament to do so. In fact, like Morselli himself (who was morbidly attached to the company of his pistol, his 'black-eyed girl'), King Umberto was marked to die by the bullet. After two earlier assassination attempts (one in the first year of his reign) he was shot through the heart by an anarchist assailant in Monza on 29 July 1900. The King's open carriage had just set out to return to the Palace after he had distributed prizes at the local Gymnastic Society. His assassin, a silk-worker, had vowed to execute him for what was not the first but probably the worst blunder of his career: the notorious telegram which he sent to General Bava Beccaris awarding him the Cross of Savoy and congratulating him on the service he had rendered 'to our institutions and to civilisation' by putting down unrest on the streets of Milan leaving 81 dead and 502 wounded.

Morselli wrote *Divertimento 1889* immediately after his hard labour on *Contro-passato prossimo*, and in keeping with the King's holiday mood and enviable disinclination to plumb the depths of his own soul this light-hearted 'entertainment' reads like a joyous vacation from its author's tragic themes and personal obsessions. They are all there beneath the good-natured surface.

Hugh Shankland, 1986

See p.ii for a list of Morselli's published works.

PART ONE
OPENING THE FAN...

———————— • ————————

I

———————— • ————————

Parasols. Parasols. Parasols. White ones, grey ones. Pink. White.

From his window they look like a river, a speckled slow-moving river of tiny domes. They have to serve as umbrellas too, for big raindrops are falling intermittently between the sunbeams streaming out of the leaden sky. For years, some say for decades, the 1st of July has invariably spelled a storm, here in Monza.

The man turns round and eyes the clock, sits down again at a desk where a tray laid across a mass of papers is waiting for him. Cheese and fruit, a bottle of wine.

He tugs the bell-pull. Without looking up he asks the aide who appears in the study doorway:

'Has *La Signora* arrived yet, from Vedano?'

No, her Ladyship's presence has not been reported.

The eyebrows lift in annoyance.

'Very well then, take her this note. In person.'

He scribbles a couple of lines. Seals the envelope, hands it to the aide.

'At the double!'

Now he can eat. Asiago cheese. Apples, pears. Plenty of bread, a few sips of wine. He has arrived very recently, his hat and travel-coat still lie in an armchair. Snack finished, he goes into the next room to freshen up. But when a man is past thirty-five he needs more than a face-wash to obliterate the effects of a fourteen-hour train journey. Next it's down to work. He pushes aside the tray, arranges the papers, adds still more from the depths of his bag. He leafs through them scanning their contents, signs none. Far too many papers, as always. A secret report from Berlin runs to a full six pages. He tosses it aside, picks it up next moment and reads as far as page 2. 'Routine stuff!' gets scrawled in the margin. The monthly report from Police Head Office looks more interesting, another four pages packed with ornate flourishes of the pen. The Minister of the Interior has seen fit to underline whole passages, and he has appended a comment of his own (twenty lines at least) which begins: *For the special attention of* . . .

Some 'highly confidential' notes from the Privy Seal, and a death penalty reprieve for signature. Two memoranda from the Minister of War. A sheaf of Royal Decrees in the red 'Urgent' portfolio. From his Personal Secretariat a bundle of private correspondence with seals still unbroken. The Mayor of Brianza has sent an Appeal: 'In view of the exceptional drought afflicting the countryside in our district of Lower Brianza . . .'

Paper, paper! 'Everything ends up as paper,' he exclaims aloud. Three-quarters of an hour's work just to get the feel of things. To take stock. A valet walks in.

'Eh? Ah yes, called Papera, aren't you. Funny thing. Nothing. Run along.'

The valet picks up the tray and disappears.

The man goes over to the window again. It is raining hard now, not a parasol to be seen. The staff are carrying tables and chairs indoors. A mighty gust of wind swoops out of the sullen sky causing a swirl of leaves and grit. The noble cedar of Lebanon, the first on the right of the main drive, bends close to breaking-point. Slap of awnings in the wind, clatter of shutters being quickly pulled to. He goes back to his desk, leaving the windows wide open: storms don't bother him. He rummages through the pile of papers again, resumes reading. The Berlin Report. Page 5: 'With his reigning grandfather now decrepit and his father incapacitated by an incurable disease, young Prince Wilhelm may very soon find himself on the throne. He is well aware of it and is preparing to assume the function which a sovereign exercises in his country, a decidedly crucial function.'

'Paper!'

'At six I'll be going out for a ride, tell them. The weather should have calmed down by then, and not just the weather. Get them to lay out my things in the dressing-room. I'll be along to change.'

He reads on: 'In conversation with a close friend the Prince is understood to have said: When my time comes I mean to revolutionise German national policy. If need be, I'll invent a new one.'

Sulphurous light flickers in the little room. There comes a rumble of thunder, followed by a sharp bang, like a shell that has found its target. The man gets up and goes to the window: the first great cedar to the right of the drive is no more, only two bare splintered stumps remain. Piles of prickly branches block the avenue, a pungent odour of resin mingles with the smell of ozone and sodden earth. The man nods his head two or three times, more in mockery than pity.

'Your turn, this time.'

No mysterious allusions, no dark presentiments. He is far too sure of his fate. Some fine dramatic death, all over in a flash? No chance. His destiny is very different, and far worse. This futile slavish job of his, condemned to trail the length and breadth of his ungrateful land – dusty, disjointed Italy – with no power and no responsibilities and yet pursued everywhere by papers and couriers, as though it all depended on him, as though he could alter a thing. Still, nothing but trials and tribulations. One headache after another. And his Household to think of, his family. Two households, two families. And himself caught between the two of them, bored stiff with both, and with his need for freedom, for seclusion. Here we go again: a light tap at the door, which he recognises instantly.

'Yes!'

And here she is, one of the two, more tactful than the other, more shrewd, yet so scathing and relentless in defending her corner. Clad in mauve and silver, the blond-as-ever braids twisted into a towering coiffure. Elegant. Radiant.

'Sit down.'

She sits. And says, as was to be expected:

'Tu es rentré de Rome, n'est-ce pas? Et je l'apprends grâce à ton aide-de-camp.'

· 5 ·

'*Le travail d'abord*,' he parries dully. 'I'm working, as you may have noticed.'

'My dear. *Toi tu m'oublies trop volontiers.*'

'And do you know what I was thinking? About this ridiculous forced labour of mine, commercial traveller-cum-pen-pusher. The moment I arrive I'm bang up against a desk.'

'Dearest, seeing you choose to resort to platitudes, may I say I am reminded of a certain colleague of yours who was famous for saying "*Toujours la reine*". You, my friend, would never say such a thing, for you it's "*jamais la reine*".'

It is not resignation or even indifference that he feels at this precise moment, simply fatigue. He fails to rise to the bait. A pause. The beautiful lady opens and shuts her fan, surveys herself in the glass behind her husband's back, lifts a hand to adjust her coiffure.

He calls her over to the window and points out the cedar.

'My God, what a frightful mess!' she exclaims with absolutely no interest. 'And to think we were all downstairs and no one noticed a thing.'

'How many of you? Two, three hundred? And not a man among you?'

'Not one man.'

And she smiles. That smile which is renowned throughout Europe, the smile which has brought comfort to cholera and earthquake victims and which first and foremost comforts herself. Herself.

The treacherous heights of Grigna had unleashed many more storms upon the lakes and fields and villas of Brianza. And many another pine, not to mention elm and lime, had been felled by lightning since that day in early summer.

Journeys and receptions, parades and processions had come and gone, and conferences and messengers, and visits by crowned heads and visits returned, and signatures and more signatures, on countless bits of paper.

One August morning in 1889. Palace of the Duchess Litta (official mistress, since time immemorial) on the Corso Venezia, in the centre of the city of Milan.

More of a fixed address than a bolt-hole, that palace. In fact the Prime Minister's special emissary had not taken long to locate his man, who was passing the time of day with wife no. 2, and present him with the latest plum from the headache-tree (as 'He' put it): viz. summons served on Colonel R* de R*, the Under-Secretary for War, by order of the Public Prosecutor in Rome. For fraud.

Case brought by an obscure veterinary surgeon answering to the name of Revagli, possessor of two dud cheques.

The Colonel's appointment, very recent like all other senior posts in the War Ministry, had been made by 'exercising the royal prerogative'. In fact it had been urged upon him by wife no. 1 and backed by various influential figures, including a Bishop. Nonetheless the initiative had been, officially, the King's, and elements of the press hostile to the Monarch and his government, to wit the greater part of the nation's leading newspapers, were gleefully blowing it up into a big scandal.

He received the envoy in the entrance hall of the palace directly after luncheon, and his good mood and post prandial cigar were extinguished at one and the same instant.

'So may one know exactly what . . .?'

Oh, simple enough. The Colonel, known as Bébé in the more exclusive Parioli clubs and dubbed 'the ugly Narcissus' in the columns of *Cronica Bizantina*, had amused himself by fixing the St Léger. The big summer race, you understand, at Le Capannelle. Through the good offices of the said vet all serious rivals to his own horse had lapped up a dose of chloral tipped into their drinking water. Brown Prince, a rank outsider, had walked away with the race, his owner with the prize-money, and various friends of his with large sums on the tote. Not so the vet, who had only received a first instalment on the full cut agreed. When the latter started to put the pressure on him, the Colonel, a compulsive spender, i.e. always rich but penniless, had actually supposed he could get himself off the hook (and he was Under-Secretary by this time, Number Two at the Ministry) by fobbing the man off with two bits of paper, a brace of worthless cheques. Not so much criminal as stupid.

The King repeated this obvious conclusion under his breath as he paced to and fro in the hallway, too depressed to rant and rage and lament his hapless fate, or even to tear a strip off the bearer of the news, the only palliative available to victims of bad tidings. He felt orphaned and deprived.

The emissary, an elderly senator, followed him with his eyes and also with genuine commiseration, as pitying as he was powerless to offer a word of comfort or advice.

'This nincompoop, tell me now, does he at least have the benefit of immunity?'

'No immunity, I regret. He does not have a seat in either Chamber. And it is not listed as an offence under Army Regulations.'

'So he will have to stand trial in open court?'

'The penal court in Rome.'

'And they'll send him to jail. To which I risk being consigned as well. Morally, that is!'

'His Majesty is entirely without responsibility . . .'

'Because I reign but do not rule, eh? And just who do you think you're trying to comfort with such asinine remarks, if you don't mind!'

The old man's pince-nez slipped off his nose, and in his efforts to retrieve it his snuff-box tumbled out of his waistcoat pocket.

But what of His Majesty, what was he to do?

In the entire Royal Household there did not exist one individual with the nerve to go and slap his face for him, that blackguard R*, in return for what he'd done to him. He had no alternative but to hold his peace, swallow the insult, lie low (over the next couple of days receive no one from Rome, open no newspapers), and meantime go straight back to Monza where he had every right to say to the Queen: 'Heard the latest? And all your doing!' Because it was the Queen who had insisted on presenting the man, this bounder of a brother-in-law of her friend Princess Saxe-Meiningen, the Queen more than anyone who had kept pressuring him for the man's appointment. Pestering him, 'crucifying' him. And now look at him, tricked and bullied, helpless and defenceless as always. And left to pick up the bill, for the sins of others.

When he arrived back at the Palace the Queen was nowhere to be found; the Mayor of Monza had invited her to the Gymnastic Society's annual gathering. So their paths did not cross until dinner, and for the moment he managed to contain his words. But not his resentment.

Dinner *en famille*; consequently in the small dining-room overlooking the Orangerie. The only guest was Countess Ghidini Servadei, lady-in-waiting, joined at the very last moment by Vinci, Minister for the Royal Household. Hotfoot from Rome, as luck would have it.

With regard to both quantity and quality of dishes it was no different to the customary evening meal: chilled salmon *purée, consommé,* sole *meunière,* chicken, tropical dessert (bananas), cassata ice. Nothing exotic, apart from the salmon, and the bananas which were a rarity. But to the King, who had only picked at the chicken, the evening's menu seemed excessive, and he remarked upon the fact to his wife. The shortest of remarks, and delivered in a tone of voice which was even shorter. 'What's all this fancy stuff in aid of? A good beefsteak and salad would do me.'

His wife was so put out that she was at a loss for words, and could only murmur a feeble: 'Whatever you say.'

She was more taken aback than offended. That the royal line of Savoy was rather frugal, at least at table, she was well aware. But this was the first time she had suffered such a rebuke in company, and on such a subject. The Ghidini woman, executing a curtsy which was closer to a genuflection, swiftly removed herself; Vinci racked his brains for some pretext to follow suit, but nothing came to his rescue. The Queen, with her husband's sanction, withdrew into the withdrawing-room, leaving the two men face to face; the one bearing disagreeable information which he would rather have imparted at some more propitious moment, the other only too aware of the fact and angrily impatient to hear what he had to say. Brushing aside Vinci's timorous suggestion of a game of billiards, the King strode onto the terrace. Then he proposed a walk in the garden.

The whole of Italy was gossiping about an electric lighting system which had been installed to illuminate all roads in the park which led in the direction of Vedano, two kilometres away. Every summer the Duchess was in the habit of paying brief visits to a villa she owned in Vedano, on the banks of the Lambro. Bean-pole Montesan they called her at Court, where she was heartily detested, the nickname alluding to her bilious state of emaciation. But those kilometres of bright lights only existed in the imagination of the malicious subjects of His Majesty, who in any case had no need of such extravagances since he possessed very good sight in the dark, another hereditary characteristic (on the Habsburg side). Consequently, when they had gone no more than a few paces from the Palace, the two men were shrouded in darkness punctuated only by the red glow of their cigars.

'Hurry up,' the King said curtly.

Vinci quickened his stride to draw level with his Chief.

'No, no. I mean out with the bad news. Because it's something tiresome that brings you here. So let's have it.'

The other proceeded to let him have it all. As Minister for the Royal Household he was responsible for the implementation of policy regarding the King of Italy's estate. Not a very enviable responsibility. Because a policy, a norm, simply did not exist, apart from the general rule of paying no regard to money whatsoever – or not at least to income, always grossly inferior to outgoings, in some years as much as thirty or even forty per cent. Either increase the one or reduce the other, that was the crux of what he had to say. The Minister had a somewhat periphrastic turn of phrase and was remorselessly repetitious; what is more, and it was most untypical of a man born and bred in Tuscany, he tended to stumble over his words. To deliver himself of his sorry little speech took him fully a quarter of an hour. And in his efforts to keep pace with his Chief who was forging ahead with great irritable strides he more than once came close to stumbling over his own feet.

'Come to the point, Excellency. The plain fact of the matter is this: I'll have to beg for bread. Expenditure, as you will appreciate, cannot be reduced. You saw for yourself just now, at table. No use trying. And that's just crumbs. So it's out with the begging bowl. Am I right?'

'I wouldn't put it like that,' said the other man. 'Still . . .'

'And I've done my share of begging already, remember. And Parliament, obsequious as ever, refused to sanction an increase in the Civil List. Twice!'

'One more try?'

'Oh no, my friend. Never again!'

'To regularise matters, if I may be so bold, there is always a third course. Not without its problems, not so very agreeable. And no more than a temporary solution, alas.'

'Ah, just hit on it now, have you? Bravo! Run up a debt. As if you had forgotten that it's already been tried. I'll say it has! The Banca Tiberina on your own recommendation, or was it the Banca Romana? Two names which mean absolutely nothing to you, I take it?'

'With respect, Your Highness, I distinctly recall at the time advising against such steps. In both cases. Other sources might have been approached, safer ones. Less exposed. The advice you took was scarcely mine.'

'Whose then?!'

'Persons to whom it was my duty to defer.'

'For heaven's sake, man!'

He turned on his heel and strode off towards the Palace. Vinci only became aware of the fact after a second or two, and had to put on a spurt to catch up with him in the dark of the night.

'And Remorini?' he heard himself being asked. 'Consulted him yet? What's his advice?'

Remorini, a mere Administrator of the Royal Properties, nominated Cavaliere for his inestimable services to book-keeping, had ever since 1880 enjoyed the Chief's particular trust and friendship.

'Remorini? Last month he tendered his resignation, in a letter addressed to yours truly, dated the 24th or 25th.'

The King's outbursts could not prevent him approaching that state in which one can no longer even bear to listen, let alone find a suitable rejoinder. He held his tongue, lashing with his walking-stick at the flowering heads of the privet which bordered the drive in profusion, scattering their delicate scent of lime. He'd had enough of attempting communication with this recalcitrant and invisible individual, more than enough. He refrained from reminding him that for quite a time that very same Remorini who had just tendered his resignation had been generally reputed to be a millionaire. Proof that Real Estate, when administered by a man who knows his job, can be highly profitable.

They returned to the Palace by way of the West Courtyard, known as the Oleander Court. The oleanders, in large copperwork flower-stands, were drawn up in three ranks before the stone staircase. At the same moment a palace Victoria carriage, complete with coachman and two footmen with folded arms mounted on the rear box, drew to a standstill in the courtyard. From it alighted a man in a soft hat, with a coat over his arm and carrying a small overnight-bag. The coach and horses wheeled away, and before mounting the staircase the traveller glanced about him. He failed to see the King and his Minister approaching between two rows of oleanders.

'Just look at that!' the King blurted under his breath. 'A coach and pair and three men for a single individual! Talk of cutting costs!'

He resolved to pursue the matter at once. On the terrace he overhauled the man and stopped him in the full glow of the gas-lamps.

'And who might you be?'

The individual, a tall well-built man of about thirty-three years of age and wearing travel-clothes of immaculate cut, did not seem to be in the least put out. Baring his head he executed a deep bow, and once he was upright again announced:

'Lieutenant Vigliotti. Orderly Officer to His Majesty.'

His Majesty's staff comprised at least ten aides-de-camp and orderly officers. Nevertheless he recognised the man.

'And where have you been?'

'On leave, sir. Three days plus travel. My pass expires tomorrow.'

'On whose authorisation?'

'C.O. the Royal Guard, sir.'

'Consider yourself in detention. Seven days!'

Vigliotti bowed low again, remaining rooted to the spot. The King hurried back down the steps, dismissed his Minister and headed for the park. No doubt to continue his walk alone. As well as possessing excellent night vision he was fond of a walk at the end of a bad day.

He saw Vigliotti again two days later, at 7 a.m. as he was coming out of the Palace for his morning gallop. The Lieutenant was waiting for him, standing by the stirrup of the second horse. He called him across.

'I placed you under arrest. What is the meaning of your presence here?'

'I was not under the impression that close arrest was intended. Under open arrest a man is not debarred from his duties. I am duty officer today.'

The Sovereign pursed his lips.

'And since when does a duty orderly report in civilian dress?'

'Naval officers on detachment to the Royal Household have permission to wear civilian dress when mounted.'

'Get going!'

Must remember to send for this chap's personal record, he thought to himself as they rode out together. He tried to recall who it was who had recommended the man. Was it the Navy Minister? Or old Admiral Brin? As for that matter of riding around in the palace coach it was obvious the man was not to blame. Someone else, somebody on the staff must have sent it to the station knowing he was due back, so as not to waste a moment. Vigliotti was a good-looking fellow. Could a woman be behind it? Only too likely. I'll get to the bottom of it, he resolved. Meantime it would hardly be fair to be too hard on the man, he'd already had one good dressing-down.

In fact he did him a favour. After the gallop and before going over to the paddock to try the jumps he gave him leave to dismiss.

'No one expects sailors to be good horsemen. I give you permission to go.'

'Thank you, sir, at your orders. But first I wonder if I might be allowed to deliver a message which may be of interest to Your Majesty? I have not had the opportunity before now.'

'Proceed.'

Proceeding was not the simplest of matters. His initiative could well appear to be overstepping the mark, bordering on unwarranted interference in the Chief's private affairs. Some justification was therefore in order, and adequate circumstantiation, even a little preamble. Vigliotti's mother's maiden name was Sprüngli, she was originally from Lucerne, and while at lady's college she had become acquainted with a German woman from Coblenz who subsequently became daughter-in-law to one of the second-generation Krupps, Erich to be exact, only to find herself a widow within a very short time. Every summer she was in the habit of passing some weeks with her old friend at the Vigliotti family home, near Monferrato.

Recently she had shown interest in one of those rustic castles which the people of Piedmont call *ricetto*, a personal property of the King. A vast mansion inhabited solely by tenant farmers and their families and fast going to rack and ruin, but set within a couple of hundred acres of coppice and woodland and commanding magnificent views. Frederika Von Goltz, the Krupp widow, had a special fondness for Italy and had quite fallen in love with Visé. When Paolo, her friend's son now attached to the Royal Household, was about to depart for Monza at the end of his leave she had urged him to inquire whether Visé might be up for sale. She was ready to pay any price for it. Any 'reasonable' price, she had hastened to add, being a practical and level-headed woman, quite ready to indulge a whim but not to be fleeced in the process. Anything but. In fact she had not failed to note that the estate was bounded on one side by the Caselli-Vercelli railway and traversed from end to end by a national highway, and consequently it had occurred to her that all those acres of scrub might turn out to have some value as building land in the not too distant future.

There existed, in short, a reasonable chance that quite apart from making her a castle-owner in Italy the woods of Visé could prove to be a first-rate investment.

II

———————— • ————————

Vigliotti had the great merit of completing all he needed to say in no more than three minutes. He was brief and to the point. He had dismounted and raised the stirrups, and now stood waiting. He knew he had taken a gamble. The Chief might very well be tempted to retort: Kindly inform your acquaintances they have no business sending people to me on such errands, only my equals deal with me directly, those beneath my station confer with my subordinates. Then there was the unfortunate incident of his return by palace carriage only two nights earlier. All the same he stood waiting respectfully, looking quite calm and collected.

And he would have felt very much more so had he had any conception of the kind of thoughts which were passing through the Chief's head.

Possessing an infallible memory for names and dates and figures, the King had no difficulty in calling to mind that property of his in the region of Monferrato, even though he had never once set foot in it. 180 hectares of land, buildings covering 10,000 square metres. What is more, he distinctly remembered someone speaking to him about it a good few years back. Who? Aha! Remorini! That traitor, that rat who abandons ship the moment she springs a leak. Years before Remorini had made him an offer for it. For Visé. H'mm. If the place had tickled his fancy then there must have been something in it for him, quite a sizeable something no doubt. Poetic justice, if that rogue had forewarned him without meaning to. Visé was worth a bit. Sell it he would, but at a price. The good lady would be made to pay through the nose for it. Half a million? Four hundred thousand? The old Von Goltz woman was very likely potty about Italy, like a lot of Germans. But one thing was for sure, he would be handling the sale himself, he wanted no intermediaries. No more blood-sucking Administrators. For once he intended to look after his own interests, directly and in person. Four hundred thousand: a very tidy sum, enough to put straight a good many things. And the Goltz woman would pay on the nail too. Were the Krupps not the richest reigning dynasty in Europe, true monarchs in their own right, not the tin-pot variety? I'll say so. A bit of good news at long last. And he would be assuming responsibility for the whole deal, nobody was going to bamboozle him this time.

Vigliotti, gloved right hand gripping the reins, forehead imperceptibly puckered, was waiting.

Being most distrusting when least necessary, like all superstitious people (and superstitious like all whom fortune seems to favour little), he told himself to 'look before leaping'. He gave orders for Vigliotti's service record to be brought to him.

From this he gleaned that Lieut. P. Vigliotti, born into a family of wealthy merchants and manufacturers, was a strict disciplinarian with his subordinates, not over-communicative or especially popular with his colleagues, professionally highly competent, 'general culture' limited. (All the better, he noted.) Aside from the Seven Seas, he had experience of navigating the far more treacherous waters of the Ministry. Physically very fit, character reserved, 'intelligence average'. (Better and better! I'm growing to like the chap.) Reports by the various superiors whom he had served under were in general agreement: no special merits or demerits. No high commendations, no reprimands, no blots on the record. 'In Society,' noted one testimonial, 'conducts himself like a gentleman, not insensible to the charms of the fair sex though always unfailingly correct; somewhat cool and reserved in his dealings with men, even with his brother officers.' He had passed out of the Naval Academy in Livorno with average points, a string of 'goods' and 'satisfactories'.

Reticent, rather stand-offish, not over-cultured or over-intelligent. Punctilious. The very man for the job. Not wanting to leave anything to chance, he called in the Commander of the Royal Guard, General Efisio Di Villahermina. All in all the General confirmed his impressions, but with a notable lack of warmth. Indeed he had one or two reservations. For instance a few weeks back Vigliotti had undeniably deviated from the line of duty, assumed responsibilities which were beyond his brief.

'Indeed? When he is no more than an orderly. Practically a batman, little more.'

'Quite so. That is why I say the man acted out of line.'

One evening in Milan, back in June. Two young officers in the Savoy Dragoons emerge from a restaurant in the centre of town. One of the two is rather the worse for drink, he starts to molest passers-by, and upon being cautioned by two policemen whacks their kepis over their ears with the flat of his sabre. Without more ado hauled off to Police Headquarters, he is charged with attempting to resist arrest and assaulting two officers of the law. His fellow officer reports the incident to his Colonel, who next morning vainly requests the young mad-cap's release. At midday the Lieutenant's immediate superior, Captain Bignardi Di Castelbignardo, orders his squadron to saddle up and at their head trots into the city where he instructs them to surround Police HQ. When the prisoner shows his face at the window of the room where he is being held in custody the dragoons unsling their muskets and hail him with the fateful battle-cry: 'Savoye, bonne nouvelle!'

It could be the prelude to an exchange of fire, Lord preserve us, between the Police and the Army. The Chief of Police loses no time in dispatching a messenger to the Prefecture, where only a few minutes beforehand the King has arrived for a state luncheon in honour of Ambassador MacIntyre who has come up from Rome to open the new Consulate-General of the United States. The urgent note borne by the messenger is addressed to the Prefect, but back at Police HQ they have shrewdly calculated that the 'bonne nouvelle' is bound to reach the ears of Someone Higher Up who will feel obliged to intervene and punish the Cavalry for the 'affront'.

Vigliotti, as a member of the royal entourage, is standing just inside the door of the Prefecture and promptly intercepts messenger and message. Without turning a hair he compels the Chief Constable to get back into his carriage and then climbs in after him. He has himself shown into the presence of the Chief of Police and persuades him to parley with Bignardi. Negotiations last half an hour, at the end of which a compromise is agreed: the Police will hand over the junior officer providing the Captain signs an undertaking that he will be severely punished. Vigliotti slips into his seat at the banquet as coffee is being served and does not breathe a word to anyone. And that is not all. Bignardi, at Vigliotti's suggestion, redeploys his squadron of Dragoons in Corso Monforte, formed up in front of the Prefecture. They can be a guard of honour, nobody will be surprised at the sight. Or any the wiser.

'That,' exclaimed the King, 'is what I call a man with his head screwed on.'

Villahermina barely suppressed a gesture of dissent. 'I am not denying the man acted promptly,' he replied reprovingly, 'on the other hand there is no question that he exceeded his brief. He might make a good politician or a diplomat, but a soldier has no time for such questionable qualities. A soldier is nothing if not upright, open and sincere.'

'He lacks sincerity, in your view?'

'I have had no dealings with the man myself. I simply draw my conclusions from the impressions of his colleagues.'

'That will be all, General.'

It was all he required to be absolutely convinced that right from top to bottom they had detected in Vigliotti an unusually able man, and one and all were after his blood. When had anyone in his entourage lifted a finger to spare him some unpleasantness? Perhaps he had exceeded his brief, no doubt he had acted peremptorily, but as a result the MacIntyre banquet had passed off without a hitch. That bunch of sheep forever getting in his way would have been only too delighted to have ruined his digestion. 'Aides', my hat! Sheep, jailors given half a chance! He had a good mind to summon Vigliotti and offer his congratulations and announce his promotion forthwith.

Careful now. Don't rush into anything, think twice for once. And take your time over this Visé business. Wait till the right moment comes up before you broach the matter again.

Well, that Vigliotti fellow had remarkable finesse. Quite remarkable: it was he who sensed the moment, more or less contrived it himself. And broached the matter in just the right light, and terms.

It happened the following Sunday. The Lieutenant was on duty again, and backing out of the Chief's study with a folder of signed documents he made bold to remark, halting in the doorway:

'If I may, sir. With regard to your property at Visé. Frau Von Goltz Krupp has charged me to inform you that the matter meets with her Sovereign's whole-hearted approval. The lady has the honour to be received at Court. The Emperor's precise words, so I believe, were: I have heard of your plan to acquire a residence in Piedmont and I approve whole-heartedly, it is one of the loveliest regions in all Italy.'

The Chief understood that he had to return the ball, after it had been delivered so adroitly.

'Ah yes now. It had slipped my mind.'

Not quite the case, but plausible. After all, he had not once mentioned the matter in the interval.

'Well, I am not averse. Upon one condition, though. The whole affair is to be kept strictly between you and me, I want no intermediaries. Is the interested party still in Italy?'

Unfortunately not, nor would she be in a position to return for quite some time. At the present moment she was in Switzerland. If the Chief so desired, he, Vigliotti, would be very pleased to attend to the matter.

'No! I repeat, no one will act in my stead. So the Von Goltz lady is in Switzerland, is she? Where precisely?'

'In Wassen, to convalesce. She recently had a bad attack of influenza. She also suffers from chronic arthritis.'

'And where exactly is this Wassen place?'

'Canton Uri, just on the other side of the St Gotthard. Right on the new line through the Gotthard tunnel.'

'Do you know the place? Any hunting?'

Vigliotti did know the place. He was not a huntsman himself, but he had reason to believe there was some shooting to be had. Chamois, roe-deer, the normal Alpine game.

'Popular spot, I take it? Villas, chalets, hotels, hot springs? People?'

Vigliotti answered with his customary fine intuition.

'Nothing, I regret to say. A few solitary mountain huts, a sawmill. Apart, that is, from the big house belonging to the lady in question. Thermal springs do exist, but they have yet to be developed.'

'And how about the rest of the neighbourhood?'

'A few kilometres higher up the road lies Goeschenen, a village with two hotels. One is rather a good hotel.'

'How many hours by train, from here?'

'Approximately four hours.'

Next morning Vigliotti left Monza with another pass in his pocket. Two days' compassionate leave. In reality, and no one else but the Chief was aware of the fact, bound for Canton Uri, on reconnaissance.

All those last days of August his family and staff were astonished to see him in such good spirits. He chatted, he smiled, he shook hands with real cordiality. His mind was set on his adventure.

Adventure? Why yes, in so far as it was a complete novelty. In his line of business the most appropriate description for time off, even a vacation, would be hard labour. On holiday at Racconigi or San Rossore he would be lucky to get three hours a day to call his own. The Royal Palace at Monza was no better than a branch office of headquarters in Rome. Journeys by land or sea, visits to friends, hunting or fishing parties, all came down to strict timetables and fixed itineraries, more or less official engagements. But this was right out of the ordinary. An incognito which was not a joke. Turning himself into Signor X or Y or Z would be like being born again, or living in a different world. And outside Italy as well, where it need not be a delusion, it might even last.

The reason for the expedition, the question of the sale, began to take second place in his mind.

Vigliotti, duly converted into his St Gotthard courier, travelled to and fro between the Royal Palace and Goeschenen, Canton

Uri. Four trips in one week. And meanwhile here was he, as thrilled as a small boy with his first part in a school play, debriefing, issuing new orders, secretly directing operations. As eager as a conscript as demob day approaches.

Back in the campaign of 1866 he had slept in empty, dust-filled country houses, in peasant cottages even, and one night actually in a tent, but he had no notion at all what it might be like to stay in a hotel. Vigliotti was compelled to report back in the minutest detail on the Hotel Adler and the six rooms which he had booked: the precise location of each bedroom, their size and furnishings, the dining-room décor, the appearance and personality of the hotel proprietor. He was dispatched back to Goeschenen to hear whether other guests were expected at the beginning of September and if so how many; and back again to check that in the first days of September the hunting season would be open and to see what licences were required. He pressed on to the canton capital to secure the necessary permits.

The secrecy surrounding the expedition naturally gave rise to a whole series of difficulties which one by one needed to be foreseen and solved in advance. He tackled them patiently, found the answer to each and every one. Never had he undertaken a journey even of the most private nature without first informing at least a dozen people, ministers and high officials, where he was bound and what route he meant to follow. These obligations were unavoidable. What was needed in the present instance was a false target, as they say in the Artillery, a fictitious but sufficiently plausible destination.

He could announce that he would be cruising to Corfu and the Aegean aboard the yacht of his good friend, Duke Di Mèlito Portosalvo. Or claim to be visiting his sister, the Queen of Portugal, staying at her summer residence on Funchal. He had to drop the idea. Too easy to check on his movements, discover the deception. Well then, a trip to Sibari and Metaponto, down south in Calabria, exploring the ruins of Magna Grecia? Again too easy to verify, aside from the fact that he had never evinced the slightest interest in archaeology, as everyone knew.

The most apt lie for the occasion is always the most banal. The simplest thing would be to make out that he was going hunting up in Piedmont, without being too precise about the locality. The mountains above Cuna, or up in the Cogne valley, towards the Gran Paradiso, or at the head of the Valle di Susa (with the possibility of straying over the border into French territory in some parts). Up there who would ever be able to track him down, ascertain whether he was there or not? Roads were few and far between, no carriages could get up that high. And to make out he was going off hunting in the Alps gave him the advantage of maximum mobility, here today and gone tomorrow.

On the other hand there was the problem of not losing touch altogether. Tricky. He turned it over and over in his mind and without consulting anyone came up with a good stratagem. Baron Guillet d'Albigny, a loyal Savoyard and second-in-command in his Personal Secretariat, would be instructed to hold the fort in Monza. If any emergencies arose Guillet would send coded telegrams to a prearranged address. Over the next half hour he amused himself hugely by devising a succinct and wicked little code in which 'Blockhead' stood for Crispi, the Prime Minister, 'Skinflint' for the Minister of the Treasury and de facto Deputy Prime Minister, Giolitti, (possibly an allusion to his austerity programme to eliminate the national debt), 'Drill Sergeant' was the Minister for War, 'Hen-House' signified the Chamber of Deputies, 'Whip-Lash' meant a royal decree. Et cetera. For members of his own family: 'Capuralèin' (little corporal, in Piedmontese) was the Prince of Naples and heir to the Throne, 'Ita' was for Margherita, the Queen. In any case, he told himself, there would probably be no need for telegrams. A courier or liaison officer could come back down to Monza every so often and bring back any urgent messages.

Count Della Gherardesca and Baron Guillet, the Head of the Secretariat and his Deputy, had not yet been let into the secret and they were consequently not a little surprised at all the agitation, although they worked tirelessly alongside their assistants to catch up on all outstanding business and get through any work which they estimated would need attention for a certain number of days ahead. He signed documents by the score, some which had not yet been written. A directive went out to Rome instructing them to take account of his impending absence.

Happily Rome from mid-August to the end of September was a dead city (or more dead than ever). They were the malarial weeks. Political life similarly came to a standstill, with both Chambers in summer recess, Embassies stripped of their Ambassadors, Ministries down to a skeleton staff, not a Minister or party-leader or lobbyist in town, and newspapers reduced to a quarter of their normal circulation.

Prime Minister Crispi had gone to Fiuggi to take the waters. Minister Giolitti was in Bognanco (province of Novara) for the same purpose. That put a very reassuring distance between the two of them.

But at Monza – the Royal Palace in the North – the customary busy social life proceeded apace, favoured by the mild air of the green Lombardy countryside (while the despised national Boot, from Bologna 'on down', languished in the savage heat of a summer which had long since bleached and shrivelled every blade of grass: that summer of 1889 was destined to go down in history as the 'African summer'). The Queen, before holidaying in Courmayeur, was holding the last of her afternoon and evening receptions, while not failing to see to her philanthropic duties, her horticultural associations and gymnastic societies, artisans' aid societies, hospitals, orphanages and old folks' homes. Her departure was scheduled for Monday, the 27th. So on that particular front he had no worries. He planned to leave on the 31st.

There still remained the Duchess, currently installed at Vedano on the banks of the Lambro, no more than ten minutes by carriage from the Palace. But 'remained' is scarcely the word, for she led the nomadic existence of the most dedicated tourist, never staying more than forty-eight hours in one place, flitting on from San Pellegrino to Castiglioncello, from Castiglioncello to Evian or Paris, or else Venice or Florence. She might be in Vedano just now, but every morning found her back in her palace in Milan frantically unpacking after the latest expedition – thirty-four pieces in all, counting each suitcase, portmanteau, shoe-bag and hat-box – and getting ready the next baggage train to accompany her to the seaside resort of Viareggio. The passion which had consumed her for years (or lustrums, rather) had never prevented her surviving happily a thousand miles from her lover, who had had no choice but to learn to survive without her, on occasions being heard to remark only slightly bitterly that for a lady (if she really is a lady) no lover's ardour can equal the attractions of a 'round trip' with Mr Thomas Cook and Company.

Passports presented a greater problem. But in the free country of Switzerland since when had anyone ever dreamed of asking a foreigner to produce a passport? Maybe so, but he felt a bit like a deserter, a traveller who was not quite bona fide. He needed to know all his papers were in order, against every eventuality. The problem arose from the fact that the issuing authority, the Foreign Ministry which would have issued the documents at a nod from him, had to be kept in the dark. Then who should turn up with perfect timing in Monza but the Minister's Private Secretary, Baron D'Invorio, on business for his master. The Baron, an ex-Ambassador, was a fellow Piedmontese and a friend of long standing. He agreed to see to everything and was as good as his word. The five passports arrived within a couple of days, in a sealed package marked for the King's eyes only.

Setting aside his own (issued in the name of Count Filiberto Di Moriana) he attended to the distribution of the other four. One went to Mancuso, his man-servant. Another to Dr Brighenti, Court Physician and his personal doctor. The third was for a certain Signor Gherardini, in reality Count Brando Della Gherardesca, who only learned at this point that he was to be included in the party.

The newly baptised Gherardini attempted to voice an objection.

'It is a great honour to be invited, but it is almost too much of an honour to be expected to travel incognito.'

'You,' retorted the Chief, 'are not just one more Mancuso or Brighenti. Thanks to Dante's story of poor old Ugolino Della Gherardesca and his cannibalism your family is better known than my own. Even to people who never got past the fourth form.'

'All the same, we are talking about a little mountain village in Switzerland . . .'

'The pedantry of professors knows no bounds.'

The fifth passport lying on the royal desk was for 'Commander' Vigliotti, expected back in Monza the following morning from his fifth mission to Goeschenen and Wassen.

All these preliminaries, every one of these preparations and precautions, was his doing and his alone – the King's. Unaccustomed to such freedom of action, to exercising so much ingenuity, he felt an inordinate pride in his achievement. Not one detail had he overlooked. To make himself less recognisable, and at the same time to stimulate his hair-growth which was beginning to show signs of wear and tear (but at forty-five who is spared?) he told his barber to shave his head as bald as an egg. His wives after all were already far removed, and up in the mountains there would be no intercourse with ladies. Apart from old Frau Von Goltz.

A rather nasty and unexpected hitch occurred at a very awkward moment, only three days before departure. Vigliotti had reported back with good news: the little hotel was half-empty and ready to welcome the party, Frau Von Goltz had been alerted and sworn to secrecy.

'Capital work, Vigliotti. And now, my dear Commander, here is your passport.'

The 'Commander' was normally more than capable of controlling his feelings, yet not even he could dissimulate his surprise. Nor, for that matter, could he have simulated it.

'His Majesty expects me to go as well?'

His Majesty's features betrayed a comparable astonishment, prompted by indignation in his case.

'What, what, what? Expect?'

'I beg your pardon, sir. I was assigned purely to the logistic side. And I was given to understand that no intermediaries were desired.'

'You are not a fool, Vigliotti. You . . . You are disloyal.'

'My loyalty is beyond question. Over three months ago I put in for and obtained thirty days' leave. Commencing the first of September.'

'Thirty days' leave!'

'On matrimonial grounds, sir. I am to be married.'

'Get out of here! And stand by for my orders.'

He was at his wits' end. The fellow was absolutely irreplaceable, no matter how junior he might be. A personal friend of Frau Von Goltz and conveyor of her offer for Visé. No one else was familiar with Visé and also with the locality where they were to meet. Moreover he was the only man among them who had a perfect command of German.

Could he be trying to up the price for his services, with this tale about thirty days' leave? Brokerage expenses?

Within the hour General Villahermina's deputy (the General was absent on his summer leave) presented him with a sheet of paper dated 15th April and completed correctly according to standing orders, whereby Lieut. Vigliotti had applied for special leave (30 days) beginning 1st September. Purpose: 'Matrimony'. The note 'Approved' initialled by Gen. Villahermina, Officer Commanding the Royal Guard, was dated 20th April. A simple orderly officer's application did not need to be countersigned by Higher Authority, i.e. Himself. In short, there was nothing to be done.

It was time to go for dinner. As he was crossing the hall at the end of the loggia which led from his personal suite of offices he caught sight of the culprit himself. In a window recess Vigliotti still stood waiting for him, ever since 5.30 when he had been thrown out, two hours alone except for two mute flunkeys positioned twenty yards apart and keeping watch on the loggia exit.

The Lieutenant did not venture to take a step towards him. He was standing to attention, a frowning dummy in severe blue uniform.

Feeling a twinge of remorse, the King called out to him:

'See me after dinner. We'll talk it over.'

'With your permission, sir. I have a plan to put to you right away, at once.'

He nodded in the direction of the footmen. The King caught his meaning, and the two men vanished at a wave of his hand.

'I am withdrawing my request for leave. I am deferring the

wedding. But I shall need to leave tonight, to go and explain things to my fiancée.'

'Capital. And who is the young lady?'

'Clara, daughter of the Marquis Mansolin, living in Padua.'

'Capital. You may have thirty-six hours.'

'More than enough, thank you. My train is at 9.15. Might I ask whether Your Majesty would object to my fiancée joining me in Switzerland? She could be accommodated in some locality not too far from where I shall be billeted.'

The Chief tickled his left earlobe with the tip of his walrus moustache. A symptom of deep thought.

'Let's think now. Would the young lady be able to keep her mouth . . .? Keep our secret, I mean to say?'

Vigliotti's face had clouded, perceptibly.

'As well as I can. Better.'

'In that case I see no objection. Can you make the 9.15?'

'I'll do my best.'

'Get hold of my Equerry, Caracciolo, and tell him my instructions are to harness Auburn and Berenice. One of my very best pairs. Before nine, long before, you'll be in Milan.'

III

———————— • ————————

'Crispi is still in Fiuggi. Giolitti is still in Bognanco.'

'Sure?' insists the Count.

Gherardesca (Gherardini) is absolutely sure. He received a telegram to that effect only yesterday.

'I don't want one or the other of them messing things up for me.'

'I guarantee there will be no bother from either quarter.'

Silence.

'You know,' the Count resumes after a little while, 'what Voltaire used to say? Monarchy is a drama more doleful than farcical.'

Gherardesca, despite his seated position, executes a little bow.

'Most erudite. Though somewhat pessimistic. My compliments, Count.'

'*Ce n'est pas de mon cru.* Margherita taught me that. My wife is very well-read, you know. She has all the classics on the tip of her tongue.'

These exchanges took place in a reserved compartment on the Rome-Basle express which had left Milan station at 7 a.m. The two men were alone in the compartment, the rest of the party being distributed about other carriages in the train. In spite of every precaution already taken and those currently operating, he still felt uneasy. When they passed through Monza, even though they were not scheduled to stop, he huddled in one corner with a handkerchief spread over his face. More excitement at Chiasso, where the Swiss customs-officials put in a brief appearance.

Then he began to grow bored. He asked Gherardesca to read him something. 'I am afraid I can't oblige,' retorted Gherardesca. 'Your instructions were to bring no books or newspapers.'

'Then read Baedeker.'

'"The railway route from Lombardy into the Swiss Alps, via the St Gotthard, constitutes a major achievement of modern engineering, bearing noble testimony to the great March of Progress that so profoundly distinguishes our xixth century, and which with the suppression of frontiers between peoples will bring about the abolition of war, poverty, ignorance, perhaps even disease . . ." "To the north of Bellinzona the line follows the river Ticino, at times traversing it by means of viaducts erected to vertiginous heights and entering an increasingly harsh and savage landscape enclosed by towering crags and dominated by snow-clad peaks, while the air becomes more fresh and permeated with the scent of pine. Between Giornico and Airolo the train burrows through the bowels of the mountains by means of numerous tunnels before reaching the great St. Gotthard tunnel itself. Several of these tunnels, despite being driven through the local *granito*, the world's hardest rock, have been boldly conceived and executed in the manner of a spiral, not unlike the winding stairway of a bell-tower . . . The traveller is at once both astonished and awe-struck upon emerging from the precipitous cliff-side to traverse a viaduct many scores of feet higher than the level at which he first pierced the mountain . . . On occasions at these lofty altitudes an eagle may be perceived flying beside the train, its peace disturbed by the noise and speed of this monster which has usurped its domain . . ."'

'Enough!'

The Count was lying stretched out on the compartment's well-upholstered divan and fanning his face with both hands.

'Damnation, it's suffocating in here! Open the window. I can't breathe.'

Gherardesca looked alarmed. He pulled down the window.

'Count, you are perspiring heavily. You have palpitations.'

'Bravo! Tachycardia at the very least!'

All the same he kept on chafing.

'Does this deuced train never stop?'

It stopped in Bellinzona. Gherardesca leapt down and ran in search of Brighenti: the Court Physician. He was in the neighbouring carriage where having laid aside his newspaper, *Il Fanfulla*, he was attempting to pursue a conversation, in German, with his sole fellow-passenger, a plump shy-looking tourist, who appeared young enough to be his daughter. A moment later 'Aesculapius', as Gherardesca privately nicknamed him, was bowed over the Chief. He unbuttoned his detachable collar, and loosened his tie.

Beneath the big fleshy nose the Count's moustache ends sagged, having lost their support or their wax.

'What the — ? Stop fiddling with my pulse. Let me get out, confound it!'

But the express had already started moving again. Well, at least there was nothing wrong with his pulse.

'Slippers! Where's Mancuso? My boots are too tight.'

The compartment opened straight out onto the track on both sides, there was no question of entry or exit until the train stopped. Seeing the valet could not be summoned, Brighenti pulled one of the Chief's boots onto his lap and started to unbutton it.

'No, leave that! Just quit fussing over me. All I need is a coffee. But of course you don't have such a thing.'

On the contrary, Brighenti had. In a flask, and still hot.

'That's what I call a real doctor,' the Chief acknowledged, lying back on his divan and sipping from the cup. 'I reaffirm my . . . complete and utter . . . confidence in you.'

'You know, to me you seem very well. Very. Maybe some small trace of nervous exhaustion, the unusual work-load of these past few days. Perhaps a very slight touch of claustrophobia. This compartment here, space is so constricted for you. But tachycardia, never. Out of the question.'

When travelling by train the Count was accustomed to having the freedom of entire carriages, with state-rooms and corridors, and servants at his beck and call. His first taste of life as an ordinary citizen was not proving a great success. Brighenti made the grave mistake of drawing his attention to the fact.

'Having your own train is a different matter altogether, so

much less tiring. For the likes of us a reserved compartment is quite a luxury, but for Your Majesty . . .'

The man sprawled on the divan suddenly sat bolt upright.

'If I hear any more such talk, or if ever you use that title again, you're going back to Monza – or straight back to Porretta.'

Porretta Bagni, the spa, was associated in the Count's mind with two very different encounters. An ill-fated one with a beautiful woman who had unequivocally rebuffed his advances (out of love, as well as out of loyalty to a husband), the other with Brighenti himself, a native of Bologna and doctor attached to the Baths. A general practitioner of no great learning, but equipped with plenty of common sense and thirty years' solid experience, Dr Brighenti had in only a few hours successfully cured him of a liver attack and had been equally appreciated for his stock of sayings in the local vernacular, and quite unwittingly for his characterisation of the beautiful lady with such exemplary scruples as 'that daft stuck-up bitch' who never tired of singing the praises of Montecatini and Vichy while running down poor Porretta, along with its waters and its climate. A month later he had found himself summoned to Rome, and before the year was out had been elevated to Court Physician and University lecturer in Hydropotology, or mineral water cures.

And now, speeding towards the St Gotthard, was he going to put his post at risk?

'No rose without a thorn, Count. The rose is your freedom. Here nobody knows who you are, you are as free as a bird, if I may so put it. With all respect, naturally. These minor upsets soon pass.'

From the divan an arm lifted in a gesture of irritation.

'They pass, I assure you. Another sip of coffee, and then by all means light up a cigar. I've noticed a puff or two works wonders for you. A little smoke never did anybody any harm.'

Meantime, as Bellinzona dropped far behind, the train was climbing towards that 'harsh and savage' landscape predicted by Baedeker, and the air blowing into the compartment was definitely becoming more Alpine. Fresh, not to say chilly. And soon it came on to rain. The Count, his collar still undone, got up and stretched his legs and then put his head out of the window for a moment. He sat down again seemingly in better sorts and supervised the manoeuvres of the other two as they hurried to shut the windows at every tunnel to keep out the smoke, lowering them again as soon as they were out. Eventually the draught blew out the paraffin lamp which illuminated the compartment in the intervals of darkness. The two men, feet planted on the seats, wrestled for a long while with the large lamp hanging from the ceiling, emptying the entire box of matches in the process. All to no avail. The lamp, a complicated contraption of brass curlicues and whirligigs, emitted one or two faint flickers and thereafter refused to do its job, so that they were condemned to total darkness just as the train entered the long tunnel itself.

Fourteen kilometres, a twenty-minute journey shrouded in deepest night. With a mixture of trepidation and high spirits they groped about, calling each other.

'Brighenti!'

'Gherardesca!'

'Count!'

Fog. Fog so thick that the headlamps of the omnibus which had conveyed them from the station to the hotel had scarcely pierced it. And so cold was it that no one later attempted to venture outside and explore. They spent the whole afternoon in the lounge before an open fire. Gherardesca and Brighenti, that is; because the Count was resting in his room, and Vigliotti had continued down the line to Wassen.

All was silent and deserted, all grey and dim. Their prognostications were equally gloomy. The Count's health, the Count's moods, the Count's probable instructions ('Pack the bags! I've had enough of this already.').

Their alarms were unjustified, or at least unjust, for he had slept for two hours as serenely as a new-born babe. Now he was lying stretched on his bed, as good as pie, gazing round his new quarters, his little pine-panelled bedchamber. Walls, floor, ceiling – all exuded a sweet fragrance, not so much of resin as of wild honey, one was almost tempted to say; and certainly it had the colour of honey, all that pinewood under its coat of copal oil. A wash-stand with flowery ewer and basin, a wardrobe sunk into the wall. That was all the furniture. Ah no, beside the bed was hung an old framed engraving depicting the Ages of Man, from childhood to old age, with tiny captions in Gothic script. And two chairs in clear white wood.

Hah! Could this simplicity actually aspire to belong to him, to possess him, even if only for a few days? Preposterous! That, more or less, was his reply – thankful, amused, and disbelieving. True, the towels were of an immaculate white, and rigidly folded. The tumblers set in their nickel rings beside the wash-stand were so highly polished that they sparkled even in the half-light of the room – making one think of a rivulet of fresh water spilling from a rock. But to sleep in here, move about, live in this room: could it really be so? And this peaceful animation around him, without a hint of melancholy, and somewhere in the background scarcely audible to him since he was a little hard of hearing, the roar of distant water (a river, or a mountain torrent?). He opened up his suitcase and got out a notebook which was normally the recipient of brief jottings of a totally practical nature, things done in the day or still to be done, impressions hardly ever, reflections never (he was not subject to them). In pencil he wrote: '*Cette petite pièce où l'on m'a confiné.*' And in his own Piedmontese dialect: '*A 'm piàs, a 'm piàs.*' I like it, I like it . . .

Gherardesca and Brighenti, down in the lounge where they were reduced to turning the pages of old numbers of the *Zürcher Illustrierte*, looked up to see him enter in slippers and dressing-gown. And they could scarcely believe their eyes. The man was actually smiling.

'So how do we go about getting a coffee?'

A waitress attired in national costume, a black skirt and a green bodice tinkling with little silver chains, brought a whole brimming jugful for him. But Mancuso was hard on her heels. '*Signor Conte*! Mind what you're doing! Too much water in it, don't touch those slops. Let me make you a proper decent coffee. I remembered to bring the Neapolitan pot.'

The Count tried to calm him: 'What if I say I prefer my slops? I'd rather you set your mind to seeing if you can rustle up a warming-pan for me tonight.' So saying, he lowered himself into a chair in front of the fire, and stayed a full hour with them, chatting about this and that. From time to time the other two exchanged looks of astonishment.

At seven he got to his feet again. 'I'll eat in my room. See I'm served by that pretty girl. Mancuso is off for the rest of the night. And the same goes for you two, naturally. Make the most of your holiday.'

Holiday? Through the windows they had been unable to discern a single house, a single inhabitant. Indoors, the entire company consisted of three elderly couples, all Swiss, whom they dined alongside without exchanging a word since Gherardesca had no German and Brighenti did not possess enough to derive pleasure from using it.

At nine, as Gherardesca was about to climb the stairs to bed, the porter hailed him with a telegram in his hand. 'There's a good start to things,' he muttered to himself. Thank God, it was only from Vigliotti, who had composed it in Wassen two hours earlier. 'Regret departure delayed. Overnighting Von Goltz. Reporting back first train tomorrow morning.'

The mist had cleared, but it was raining heavily next morning when the Count looked out of one of the little windows (his broad shoulders filled it completely) in the room where he had slept. Below, in the meadow behind the hotel, he saw Mancuso gesturing to a trio of bearded men in leather shorts and heavy boots and holding metal-tipped sticks. Two beaters and a porter engaged previously by Vigliotti for the hunt. He dressed and went down to them. Mancuso, a native of Aspromonte in the highlands of Calabria, was an experienced hunter of wild boar and roe-deer. He was getting on well in sign-language, except that he was of the opinion that bad weather brought the larger game closer to inhabited areas and therefore it made sense to begin the beat right there and then, whereas the three locals disagreed, indicating it was best to wait and in any case it would be dangerous for their employers to go up high while there was any risk of cloud. That dialogue between mutes, conducted entirely in mime, entertained him for quite a while. In the end he dismissed the three Swiss and told Mancuso to accompany him on a preliminary reconnaissance of the area. Beneath a gigantic red umbrella borrowed from the porter they set out along the highroad which comes down from the pass and describes a large S in the middle of the village as it crosses the ravine through which the Reuss flows.

Or rather, where the Reuss gives the appearance of ceasing to flow. Seen from the old stone bridge, the river far below looks green and deep, as placid as a lake. The Count lingered at the parapet on the pretext of trying to gauge the height of the drop: thirty metres, possibly thirty-five; but really to make sure that he did not feel giddy, one of the signs of the onset of the male mid-life crisis, so he had been told.

Apart from the *Gemeindehaus*, or village hall, there was little more to the hamlet than a few humble dwellings built of stone and timber, the timber so weathered it looked like stone, the post-station for the St Gotthard diligence, a *Bäckerei* or baker's shop, and one or two other dusty little stores which gave him the opportunity to relive an almost forgotten experience: shopping.

Handing over your money, pocketing the change, behaving like other people do so enviably every day . . . He bought stamps, and postcards which he would never send, chocolate he would never eat because it was against doctor's orders, a half-bottle of Kirsch which he presented to Mancuso, exactly like a real-life tourist who has to count every Swiss franc he spends.

As he entered the hotel again Vigliotti stepped up to him and made his apologics.

'What for?'

For having had to spend the night in Wassen, at Frau Von Goltz's residence; landslips caused by the heavy rain had blocked the carriage-road, no diligences were running. Accordingly he had had to wait for a local train next morning, international trains did not stop in Wassen.

'You could have stayed longer if you wanted. There's absolutely no hurry.'

'With reference to our negotiations, the lady is honoured to communicate . . .'

'Let's leave that till later, shall we.'

'Excuse me, sir, but I may not be here later. I really ought to meet the eleven o'clock train. Signorina Mansolin, my fiancée, is arriving at eleven and with your permission I should like to accompany her to Andermatt. All being well, I should be back by nightfall.'

'Why so far?'

'Your instructions, Count.'

'Mine?'

'Following a suggestion of mine. For reasons of discretion.'

'Look here, is your fiancée travelling alone or does she have a chaperone?'

Signorina Mansolin, he was informed somewhat punctiliously, was not unaccompanied. She had been entrusted to the care of a lady companion of mature years, her ex-Governess, Frau Schwartz, who had been in the family's employ for a great many years.

'Well then, why not bring her straight here? The hotel is perfectly comfortable, and almost empty too, and I'm sure you'll find there's all the room you could need.'

Unlike a great many Swiss hotels at that time, there was no *table d'hôte* or common dining-table at the Hotel Adler.

Each guest or group had a separate table beneath the low coffered ceiling ('AD 1611' according to a painted scroll) in the dining-room into which the daylight filtered through lattice windows (similarly inscribed and dated) to make the walls glow a fine shade of salmon pink, the typical patina acquired by seasoned *abies retica* sawn into thick panels, a speciality of the region. The timbering and the leaded windows were reminiscent of a church sacristy or Gutenberg's workshop, and yet the overall effect was homely and cheerful. The staid oak chairs were comfortably softened by green and yellow cushions, the window-sills were enlivened by red geraniums. The tablecloths were embroidered with rhododendrons, the polished jugs and glasses sparkled invitingly.

The room was not especially large. From one end to the other the diners had a clear view of each other, and no difficulty in hearing one another's voices. The Swiss (or German or Austrian) couples emitted a decorous murmur. The Count and his company, seated by the windows, contributed more robust tones, in the Italian fashion. At the other end of the room where the huge porcelain stove snored to itself a youthful female voice, not markedly euphonious, fluctuating between hushed-conspiratorial and piercingly shrill, kept up a monologue in Italian and German with a lady in a black wig and lace bonnet whose most immediate concern seemed to be to do justice to the local cuisine. (Plain fare of not the most mouth-watering nature, as the Florentine Gherardesca and the Bolognese Brighenti observed somewhat apprehensively.)

Having finished her first meal in Goeschenen, Clara Mansolin, leaving Frau Schwartz to wait for her coffee, rose from table and with gracious modesty withdrew from the room, not without bestowing in the Count's direction the hint of a smile and a curtsy, both so finely executed as to be perceptible only to the recipient.

'If I may be permitted an indiscretion,' he said leaning towards Vigliotti, 'how old is the Signorina?'

And on learning that she was twenty-one:

'She looks three or four years younger. Well, if you wish to join her, please don't stand on ceremony.'

'Would the Count be agreeable to discussing the Von Goltz matter for just one moment? The lady is most anxious to be received by you. She has to return to Germany in a few days' time. For the wedding of her only great-niece.'

No peace for the wicked. Duty calls, even here.

'Very well, I shall expect Frau Von Goltz at eleven tomorrow morning. See to it she is informed. I'm anxious to get this business over and done with too, tell her, even more than she is.'

The world, for him, had always divided into Good and Bad, and no matter how many allowances were made he had never been able to put up with the host of things which he was incapable of enjoying. Horses were Good (his 'teams', the famous fours which were the envy of the Prince of Wales), women too, and the army – barracks life and manoeuvres, but not parades – and money was another good thing, of which he was wont to say: 'Filthy lucre; shame I enjoy spending it.' Everything else, without exception, was equally insufferable.

Politics and politicos, culture and culture-mongers, art, music and painting (the time-honoured philistinism of the Savoys), Dame Nature in her non-horsey and non-hunting guises, trees and flowers and sunrises and sunsets, all very fine for women and poets, pomp and etiquette, ceremonies of any description, court, military, academic, or whatever. This rudimentary Manicheism was reinforced by a penchant for generalisation, typical of a shallow mind, whereby all experience, of necessity long and varied in a man of his age and station, could be summed up in a few pat phrases, the crassest of maxims and *bons mots*. Women? Fads, fashion, fanny. Steer clear of the three Ps: priests, procurators, professors.

Many, far too many, were therefore the things which one had to be on one's guard against. Papers, for one thing: all archives, documents, ledgers, pacts, contracts . . .

The next morning he was greeted by Gherardesca who conducted him to a private room on the first floor containing a table covered with land-registry maps and old yellowing deeds carefully displayed for his perusal.

'You want to make me detest this little hotel where I was actually hoping to have a nice time.'

He sank into a chair, exhausted before even starting.

'Get me a coffee and my glasses.'

Inspection of the papers lasted half an hour. At eleven o'clock the Count stepped out onto the balcony wearing the bored and sullen expression of a schoolboy in exam-time. At the same moment a carriage swung off the highroad and drew up in front of the Adler.

First out was a portly gentleman in frock-coat and top hat with a briefcase clamped under his arm. Next emerged Vigliotti, followed by the tall, slender figure of a woman of about thirty-five dressed in hunting-garb with a beaver cap perched hussar fashion on her brown locks. The man with the briefcase remained standing rigidly beside the carriage, while the other two climbed the steps into the hotel. A moment later the visitor was saying, in excruciating French:

'Good morning, Count. I am honoured to be able to pay my respects.'

Who the deuce was this woman? He signalled to Vigliotti to step out into the corridor a moment.

'Well? What's happened to La Goltz?'

'Frau Von Goltz, widow of Erich Krupp the younger. That's her in there.'

'That? Didn't you tell me to expect an old lady?'

Vigliotti affected surprise. Never had he said anything of the kind. To the best of his knowledge La Goltz was in the region of forty years of age.

'How can it be? When among other things you told me she was a great-aunt and due to attend her grand-niece's wedding?'

'The grand-daughter of her eldest brother, Hermann Von Goltz.'

'It's beyond belief!'

Preliminaries and negotiations, as he desired, were completed very quickly. In the course of it two things in particular impressed themselves upon him: that his incognito was most scrupulously respected, and that 'blood will out'. Vigliotti, scion of one of the biggest industrialists in the entire region of Biella, conducted negotiations like a master.

Speaking in German and translating phrase by phrase as he went along he explained that the Count was prepared to contemplate the sale of Visé as a special favour towards the lady and in recognition of Emperor Wilhelm's evident wish that the purchaser should be Frau Von Goltz in particular. And then he bluffed boldly:

'The Count's Administrators have advised against ceding the estate. Land and property prices are currently reacting to the appreciable increase in investment in that area of the market consequent upon the recent crisis of the Bourse. That is to say, they display an upward trend which in all probability will be prolonged. Hence their advice is to wait. Nevertheless the Owner has agreed to accede to the lady's request, for the reasons already given. Furthermore he is prepared to part with it at a very favourable price. Eight hundred and ninety thousand.'

This figure, to judge by the way her eyebrows shot up, had

evidently not been previously disclosed to the intending buyer. And the Count himself, truth to tell, was flabbergasted. All the same he was wise enough not to let it show. But mentally he said to himself: the man's got no sense of proportion, he's going to lose me the whole deal.

'Negotiable,' conceded Vigliotti.

As for terms of payment: a down payment of 100,000 liras upon signature of the precontract. A further 100,000 payable within thirty days, the balance of the sum contracted to be delivered directly to the Vendor within a period not exceeding three months.

La Goltz broke her silence to point out that she would be unable to travel to Italy in that period.

'You are free to grant power of attorney to anyone of your choosing,' retorted Vigliotti. 'There is no need to trouble yourself in person.'

'I shall need to confer with Herr Grüber.'

The gentleman, naturally, who had remained by the carriage – her factor and financial adviser. He was duly summoned upstairs, and the three Italians withdrew.

When the conference with Grüber was over, Vigliotti went back into the room. He re-emerged to say that the lady was prepared to sign the precontract there and then, provided the Vendor would generously oblige her by dropping the price to seven hundred and fifty thousand.

Well, it was still one and half times more than anything he had ever dreamed of raising. The Vendor lost no time in giving his assent. The text of the contract of agreement having been prepared in advance, all that was required was to fill in the appropriate sums and dates, and sign; all of which was speedily accomplished. One hundred notes of the *Banca d'Italia*, each to the value of one thousand liras and bearing the Cross of Savoy watermark, were counted out by Grüber and collected by Gherardesca.

After a glass of vermouth, and well before noon, the beautiful Frau Von Goltz was on her way back to Wassen.

Beautiful? He was not entirely sure. The Amazon style, the Valkyrie look, did not particularly appeal to him. The eyes, now they surely were beautiful; though with something just a little unsettling about them, a reaction which it goes without saying he made not the slightest attempt to fathom.

He felt much more sure about the sale which had just been concluded, the one hundred thousand in cash. Nothing like it, it was the speediest and most lucrative deal he had ever brought off in his life. Just one question lingered in his mind: that extraordinary fellow Vigliotti, what motives could the man really have? The Count had never entertained any illusions about the disinterestedness of his staff. So what was he after, this young Vigliotti? A big commission, that went without saying. He had not the faintest notion what percentage was due to a broker in a case like this, but even supposing Vigliotti was only banking on taking a twentieth of the price agreed, and after all it would be a pretty fair slice of the cake, it still struck him as rather odd that he should be satisfied with that and nothing else. What was the real reward that Vigliotti was after, what ambitions was he concealing?

Well, time will tell. Meanwhile he got Gherardesca to pen a couple of lines to him. 'Dear Vigliotti, I am most obliged to you for the part you played in my negotiations with Frau Von Goltz, successfully concluded today with the sale of the estate of Visé, and I mean to see that you receive prompt and tangible expression of my appreciation.'

Gherardesca caught the 16.15 train for Monza, with Brighenti in escort. His mission was to deposit the sum received, too substantial to be stored in a hotel wardrobe, and both men were to report back within twenty-four hours. Before departing he asked the Count whether there were any messages to be passed on, any orders. 'Nothing! Now I am going to treat myself to a rest. I think I've earned it, don't you? And you're not to bring any papers back, let's be clear about that. You just tell them to leave me alone. The whole lot of them!'

IV

———————— • ————————

The rest of the afternoon, after the other two had left for Italy, was destined to have a special place in his memory for a long while. 'I discovered life.'

He went out for a walk. Nothing more adventurous than the main road. Entirely alone. In the yard outside the Adler coach-house they were rinsing down the hotel omnibus with great pailfuls of water and its brilliant glossy red shone like a sweet-tin. In the village the weekly market was packing up. But under the *Bäckerei* between the twin flights of stone steps running up to the shop a coppersmith's wares were still on display, pots and pans and jugs, like so many little suns arrayed to tempt the true one to show its face.

Girls up from the valley of the Reuss with baskets of bilberries and cyclamen still had things left to sell, laid out beside them in the backs of carts where they sat, in their black flower-embroidered skirts and white stockings, their legs dangling. He was alone, praise God, in the midst of these people who knew nothing of him. No escort, no bodyguard, no police commissars clumsily got up as civilians for a man who normally could go nowhere without outriders and a whole 'train' of swallow tail-coats and kepis festooned with gold braid – guarded, insulted, assaulted, or acclaimed and showered with flowers. He felt no temptation to take the mountain road, happy to promenade up and down between the hotel and the post-station, passing the occasional tourist armed with guidebook and binoculars or country folk making their way home from market or returning with full panniers from their mountain-pastures. All the foreign visitors stopped to greet the sun when at long last it pierced the clouds and lit up the curving Goeschnerthal, black with pine forests, and the icy slopes of the Dammastock ascending into vaporous blue. Not he. Nothing existed outside that private happiness of his.

When it came to dinner, he was alone again. Vigliotti, with his leave, took a seat at the Mansolin table. In the entire dining-room there were no more than ten clients including themselves, but service proceeded at the most leisurely pace. The two little waitresses kept him waiting a quarter of an hour after removing his soup-plate, and all that time he sat thrilled to be made to wait.

The evening, in any case short since those good folk were in the habit of going to bed by ten (that night the Count went as early as nine), concluded in the most agreeable fashion.

'Join me in the next room, my friend, and ask the young lady if she would care to come along too.'

In all likelihood Vigliotti was not unduly surprised at the cordial invitation (he had earned it), but he must have marvelled at the bravura with which his young Clara acquitted herself at her début. Humouring Signor Moriana was often no simple matter even for an expert, and in the present situation, even though the formalities had been relaxed, his incognito could by no means be said to sanction familiarity. Clara, assuming her convent-school look and demeanour, conducted herself with noteworthy aplomb. Her replies were succinct, she discreetly proposed two or three perfectly judged topics of conversation (the awfully over-praised beauty of the Swiss Alps, the frightful risks attendant upon hunting in the mountains, with just a hint of admiration for the hardy hunters), and she refrained from asking questions. Except once. The Count had slipped in a personal reminiscence of the war, and Clara had promptly exclaimed: 'Oh, what war?' – a reaction which suggested that her knowledge of patriotic history left a lot to be desired, or else that she did not suppose him old enough to have taken part in battles (back in '66) fought before she was born. The Count, whichever of these hypotheses he preferred, grinned broadly.

He toasted her and her fiancé. Oh, just a drop of kirsch. He had

had half a mind to order champagne, but then reflected it would not be right to make too much of the morning's success.

'A country suffering from chronic rain,' had been Dr Brighenti's diagnosis of their holiday place. And next morning it was raining again.

It did not seem to matter to the Count. He got up very early and on his own went straight to wake Mancuso. They were going hunting, he announced; just the two of them, no one else. What was this, had his man allowed himself to be converted by the beaters? Mancuso ventured to point out that they wouldn't be able to see more than a yard in front of their noses, what with all that thick cloud hanging about the valley. '*Que l'diable emporte le diable!*' countered the Count, employing the heroic motto of one of his forebears at the siege of Geneva. And forth they set.

By about ten o'clock, having climbed to around 1800 metres, they were above the thickest lower levels of cloud and visibility improved considerably, although even at that height rain still kept falling. The occasional cluster-pine, bracken, broom, rhododendrons – they had reached the hunting reserve. Difficult terrain, even in fair weather, studded with huge boulders and scored by ravines. Mancuso led the way without speaking, vainly seeking something to give them cause for hope in that unfamiliar world.

The trail seemed an interminable slog to both men as they picked their way across the mountainside in that chaos of slippery rocks and tangled tough vegetation which made every step an effort. The Count sniffed the air as noisily as a bloodhound. He huffed and puffed. At last Mancuso stopped dead in his tracks, signalling to the Boss to stop as well. He was crouching down, evidently having detected something unusual: the tops of some of the taller shrubs had been freshly bitten off. And there was a stream close at hand, to judge by the sound – another good sign. In summer larger animals never stray very far from running water.

Mancuso dropped to the ground and began emitting a curious melancholy call. Like the whining of a new-born baby or the whimper of a puppy. He would stop for a while, and then softly begin again. This went on for a not inconsiderable time. The Boss, also stretched full length on the boggy ground and shivering and soaked to the bone, was beginning to lose patience. He was just about to get to his feet when his eye was drawn to a yellowish brown bush, some hundred paces uphill from where they lay. Very softly the bush shook, and then took a step forward. It was an animal of some sort. Tawny coat, much larger and more thickset than a mountain goat; and it kept on coming their way. They were downwind, so it could not be aware of them. The Count raised his rifle and took aim (nervously and too quickly).

'Drat!' escaped Mancuso's lips.

The animal, not even grazed by the shot, sprang into a thicket of broom and made off fast in the direction of the stream, presumably to put water between itself and its enemies. But a poor beast is no match for the lure of death. Suddenly it doubled back and showed again, then bolted downhill across the slope. Straight to the spot where Mancuso was waiting for it. It leapt above his head and all he had to do was raise his right arm with the knife-point uppermost. Like a rent curtain it flopped to the ground after a few paces, and Mancuso finished it off with an accurate, even merciful blow, a sharp-pointed stone banged hard between its eyes. It was a large male steinbock with small delicate tapering ears which contrasted startlingly with the massive un-branched horns as hard and gnarled as briar roots.

There had been nothing very exhilarating about their achieve-ment; Alpine creatures are the least wary of all, because of their limited acquaintance with the human animal. The look which the two men exchanged contained no hint of triumph. Besides, there was no question of their being able to carry their prey down the mountain. Game of that size is transported by suspending it from a pole run between its legs tied together front and back. They did not have the means. Mancuso removed his loden jacket and then his shirt and pulling down the top of a spruce fastened his shirt to it. A sign to help him relocate the spot where the steinbock had begun his long sleep. In his own kingdom, which had not protected him.

They needed to get back, and it promised to be no easy matter.

The valley was dotted with cloud again, one large one clinging to the mountain just below them like a fungus to the bark of a tree. Heading straight downhill they experienced the mythological adventure (comical to anyone who had seen them) of stepping onto a cloud and vanishing from sight. Just like that, one after the other, like Mephistopheles dropping through the trap-door in a stage. And at once they were totally lost. The Count walked straight into a gigantic boulder. In the collision his gun went off, and the bullet came within a whisker of passing through his leg. Things became even worse when in the murk the close-set tangle of pine-trunks began again, on a 45-degree slope. That thick, brittle undergrowth of mastic and myrtle, bilberry and dwarf juniper, in which you founder and flounder conceals a treacherous scree made up of big round slippery stones. Every wearisome step is a snare for those unused to such terrain, and backbreaking work. Your leg is gripped to the calf and before you manage to tug it free the other is sinking as well, the foot snarling or slipping or twisting between or over the stones, all of them invisible and vicious as the jaws of a man-trap. The Count damned and blinded. He swore that never again would anyone induce him to go up there, he'd sooner go hunting among the glaciers. Whenever they stopped the stillness of the mountain was penetrating, which he hated. He had been known to say he found it more deafening than a twenty-one gun salute.

It might have been about two in the afternoon, and without a doubt they had been a good couple of hours struggling downhill in that gruelling torture, groping blindly from pine-tree to pine-tree, when they felt the ground tremble underfoot and at the same time heard a deep dull rumbling. Then the far-off whistle of a locomotive. Somewhere directly below them must be the end of a tunnel, thank the Lord. And in time they reached it, slithering on their backs over the last stretch down the railway cutting to fetch up in the ditch beside the line, waist-deep in icy water but safe at last. The long march after that was a relief in comparison, all they had to do was keep following the tracks, though where they were leading them they had no idea, having lost all sense of direction. Rain began falling again, fairly pelting down. They did not even notice that they had crossed a viaduct until they were on the other side of it. But after the viaduct they sighted a signal up ahead. Then points. And at long last a station: Wassen.

It did not surprise them, for they felt as though they had been walking for a week. But they were startled at the look of astonishment on the faces of the people at the station: the original colour of the clothes on their backs was anyone's guess, and of the boots on their feet only the uppers were left. The soles were torn to shreds.

Trains back? Nothing before seven. A carriage? No carriages. Not even the St Gotthard mail-coach was running, another rockfall had blocked the highroad.

The station-master spoke Italian, and he sat the luckless pair in front of a glowing stove in his office. Mancuso began to revive, after a hunk of bread and some coffee. The Count needed a lot more than that. A good hot bath, for a start.

Wassen, he thought to himself. Wassen means Von Goltz. He could go and knock on her door. Mancuso was given instructions to wait for the seven o'clock train and get back to Wassen as fast as he could, that same evening, with a change of clothes.

He found it was quite a climb up the road before he sighted the gates of the Villa Goltz, emblematically perched on a solitary rocky eminence. Its fiery red shutters stood out boldly against the dark-stained timber walls, under a roof of granite slabs: a perfect replica on a wealthy middle-class scale (twenty-two rooms) of the humble mountain chalets of the Bernese Oberland. The owner of this elephantine hut betrayed no surprise on discovering that crowned and bedraggled pilgrim on her doorstep.

'Ce sont des imprévus bien prévoyables. Et pas tellement affreux,' she confined herself to observing.

She apologised for greeting him in her work clothes, her smock and gloves. In her *atelier* she had been carving a raven out of a block of pine, three times life-size. She devoted much time to the production of similar *objets d'art* and in the living-room a large number were on display: eagles, nocturnal birds of prey, marmots, squirrels, a fair sample of Alpine zoological specimens hacked out by her roughly but effectively, with mallet and chisel. She was a society woman, very much so, but for one month in the year she chose to retire to her mountain retreat and pursue a solitary, even contemplative, life; with five servants, and no guests or callers. She had no wish for them. An intelligent woman, she was of the opinion that the mountains either assimilate or repel, and she chose to be assimilated. Back home, in Berlin, she led a leisurely and indolent life, but here she took long walks or else worked, often the whole day through, an excellent remedy for arthritis. At home she was a superficial person, here she liked to delve into things (or at least into what was available); at home, like any other *bonne bourgeoise*, she was a listless and passive lover, but up here she came to life again. In the company of a certain Joseph Rappen, herdsman and *Bergführer*, or mountain guide, she tackled arduous climbs in the Dammastock range, and in Wassen it was said that Rappen also served her for other exploits, of a more intimate nature. She made no attempt to scotch the rumour. Largely because it was the plain truth.

She took the Count up to the first floor of the villa and left him in the care of a valet. The room was vast and furnished in the old style of the valley, but he was gratified to note that it was heated by radiator and had a bathroom attached. Ten minutes later he was stepping out of a forty degrees bath, a new man. The valet awaiting his orders went off at once to fetch him a plate of fried eggs and a glass of port. He ate quickly, and then slipped into bed and slept for three hours. A sleep so deep and so fulfilling that to experience the same, every day of the year, he would have parted with the throne of Italy without a single regret.

Beside the bed when he awoke at seven o'clock he discovered slippers, underwear, a padded dressing-gown and a silk cravat. All brand new, and each article suiting him perfectly. He was so delighted to put on these things after his blissful sleep that he did not think to ask himself how such garments came to be in the home of the widow Goltz. He simply accepted everything, as pleased and incurious as the hero in a fairy tale.

They dined together, not in the large dining-room below, but by soft lamplight in an upstairs chamber only a few steps away from the room in which he had slept. The mistress of the house, exhibiting the most exquisite tact, herself appeared in déshabille, a short-sleeved night-gown with her dark hair loose over her shoulders. No jewels. Only her eyes.

This time, gazing into them with awkward diffidence, he judged them to be large.

Large they were not. But equally they were not so small. A fine mouth, a good figure, can be assessed at a glance; but the size of a woman's eyes, if they happen to be beautiful, is notoriously difficult to divine (aside from what is hidden behind them). In this instance they also varied in colour, gold-flecked and turning from green to stone-grey, precious stones that changed their hue not merely in response to the play of light in the room. They could dilate with a kind of laughing intensity which was the reverse of innocent or even charitable, and not always even very pretty or proper. Eyes which quite openly enjoyed the paradoxes inherent in certain situations, and appreciated their comical side. Highly expressive of irony, even straightforward derision. Fortunately for him, the Count was made of coarser stuff, altogether different, and these nuances escaped him.

On the other hand he fully appreciated the supper, speedily served and presided over with liturgical solemnity by a butler as refined as Edward Prince of Wales and as sober as Gustav Rothschild. No dessert, no ice cream, but an excellent selection of fruit, just as he preferred. Champagne of that precious *cru* of '72 which so handsomely compensated connoisseurs for abstinences endured during the Franco-Prussian War. Between dishes, though this was somewhat less to his liking, La Goltz drew clouds of smoke from a pipe *à la* George Sand, through its two-foot long silver stem.

At length the staff withdrew, leaving them to themselves. Although he felt flattered at the prospect of the probable epilogue to the evening he also viewed its approach with a certain apprehension, on account of his earlier exertions. When the time came he acquitted himself with honour (without being aware which of them had actually taken the initiative, the lady had given herself so freely and naturally). His labours could scarcely be said to be Herculean, but they were exhaustive. And contrary to his normal habit quite discriminating, with admirable refinements of self-restraint and delay.

He adapted himself to the grace, and the intelligence, of the body moving with his own. Only later did he come to understand he had submitted to that superiority, and for this he bore her a proper, male, resentment.

Mancuso and suitcase turned up next morning at eight. No 'big scene' over the delay (unavoidable). The Boss greeted both with a smile. He had, once again, slept beautifully. Like a Senator through a debate, as he was fond of saying.

He was writing. Verbatim: 'Most grateful for the handsome hospitality and hoping to be able to return it very shortly. Yours . . .' To have enjoyed the favours of a woman who only the day before had paid him 100,000 in cash had something deliciously equivocal about it, especially for someone who was generally the one to pay (and dearly). Dashing off a couple of lines in his own hand spared him the usual tiresome formalities and her any possible embarrassment. In short, he calculated on being able to slip away 'without fuss'. They had a train to catch at nine.

A miscalculation, as it turned out. Because just as they started down the front-door steps they saw, in the middle of the fore-court, the lady herself in the act of mounting the back of a mule, and being given a leg up by a young man dressed in fustian and hob-nail boots. Rappen, the mountain guide.

She wore trousers too and sat astride the beast.

'Madame, I am really most deeply obliged. Indeed I ask myself how I can ever adequately . . .'

'*En vous obligeant encore une fois, Monsieur l'Comte!*'

Civil enough, but rather perfunctory. And how come she now spoke the most perfect French? For the meeting over the Visé sale Vigliotti had been needed as interpreter. Devilish mysterious.

Outside Goeschenen Station he bumped into Gherardesca and Brighenti. Back from Monza the night before, they were about to board the train again for an excursion, complete with binoculars round their necks and white Panamas on their heads, despite the sheeting rain. They planned to have a look at Lake Lucerne. Both were profuse in their apologies, justifying themselves by explaining that they had entrusted Vigliotti with a full written statement confirming the safe deposit of the 100,000 lire. Actually, they had not been expecting to see the Count back quite so soon.

'Oh no?'

'Well, this shocking weather.'

'Hardly so shocking, if it gives some people ideas of going off on a jaunt.'

Actually the full plan, providing it met with his approval, was to overnight in Lucerne and be back not so very late in the morning.

'By all means stay away, if you want to,' was his jovial reply.

'You,' said Brighenti to Gherardesca once they were safely installed in the train, 'are so ungrateful that you'd not give him any credit for that "if you want to". It shows that he recognises the fact that we have our rights too and when it comes down to it, by Jove, we're all of us on a par, the King and his subjects!'

'And you,' rejoined Gherardesca, 'are so far gone that you fail to appreciate that when he says "Stay away" what he really means is "Make yourselves scarce, you jackasses!"'

'He', meanwhile, was strolling downhill towards the Adler beside Mancuso, greeting each tree, each stone, as though he were returning home again. At the entrance, leaning against the doorpost, stood Herr Wüntz, the proprietor. A big heavily-built man with grey mutton-chop whiskers who, apparently having nothing better to do, spent his days occupied in that way watching who passed on the road and who went in and out of his establishment, acknowledging his clients with a sly wink, no more. Indolent as a Neapolitan, the Count thought to himself, and just as likeable. And he gave him a smile. That morning he smiled upon the whole world, without distinction. Finally Mancuso was released as well, eager to get back up the mountain and retrieve 'the beast', as he called it, still lying up there rotting under the rain.

Why, of course, 'his' steinbock. 'I'll send it down to Monza for Ghirindelli to stuff,' he thought privately, 'and then I'll present it to the Duchess.' Capital idea. Meantime he himself was going nowhere near the place, nobody was posting him back down there, touch wood, not even stuffed. Herr Wüntz and his little hotel, that was the life. And he told himself not to count the days, poor devil, those he had enjoyed and those still to enjoy. Their number was shrinking fast, they were becoming ever fewer and more precious, to be uncorked and savoured one by one, minute by minute.

And just let anyone try taking them away from him!

And then off the eleven o'clock train from Italy, totally unexpected, stepped Guillet d'Albigny, Gherardesca's Deputy in his Personal Secretariat. This time he was anything but jovial.

'Now what? Come to steal the air I breathe?'

Had Gherardesca not sworn that nothing of any importance had come up in Monza?

'Quite so, sir. However an officer arrived from Naples yesterday evening detailed to bring you a letter. He says it's very urgent. And also I thought it not inexpedient to . . .'

Generally speaking, the young man down in Naples did not cause him any headaches. So what the deuce was happening? What was happening, so the Very Urgent letter disclosed, was the Regimental Day, the regiment of which he was Colonel-in-Chief, as well as the oath of loyalty, no less, of the young man's second intake of recruits. Papa was urged to attend, the two solemn events being arranged for the same day, 20th September, the anniversary of, etc.

Guillet had thought it not inexpedient to avail himself of the opportunity to bring along a small portfolio of correspondence to be 'disposed of'. So the Count was obliged to seat himself at a writing-desk in the private room on the first floor and read, listen, sign, dictate. And write. To his son he wrote at quite some length: 'A man who should know what he is talking about, and who knows and likes you' (this was the General commanding the Army Corps under whose jurisdiction the young man was amusing himself by nit-picking and earning himself a reputation throughout the regiment as an ogre) 'was recently telling me that recruits consider it a disaster to end up under your command. We folk with crowns where ordinary people have hats are instinctively resented by everyone or almost everyone, and so we make a point of rendering ourselves truly insufferable, we positively revel in it. But mark my words, it is a trait that can cost us dear, remember Great-Grandpapa. Your chaps come from Battipaglia and Altamura, not from Pomerania, and if ever you hear them say "I don't go for the bloke" think twice before clapping them in irons.' After these tips, indisputably the fruit of genuine experience, he appended a PS. 'I'm making no appointments for the 20th, I don't doubt I have quite enough lined up already.' He wrote to his wife too. 'Hunting proceeds, without great success. Always on the move, regret unable to give you any precise address. But sleeping well, health good. Trust the same goes for you in Courmayeur.'

He took a bite to eat, right there in the room with Guillet, and kept hard at it.

He was impatient to get through it all and be rid of the man. The man, of course, was innocent, and even 'not inexpedient', as he kept trying to tell himself. And still he wished him to the devil, despite his own wise words about being more tender-hearted towards one's conscripts.

'You don't want to miss that train. It's at 4.15, and don't forget.'

Before it struck four they were through, everything was disposed of. He did the 'air-thief' the honour of accompanying him the whole way to the station, so keen was he to see the back of him and all he stood for. Guillet (formerly a Lieutenant in the Guards and his comrade-in-arms on the field of Villafranca) awkwardly stammered his thanks, only too honoured and only too aware that every instant of that half-day his lord and master had detested him from the bottom of his heart.

V

————————— • —————————

Having exorcised the black apparition in the topcoat he still had three hours left until dinner. A wealth of time.

He could retire to his room, or mingle on the terrace with the votaries of Thomas Cook squinting at the misty peaks of the Dammastock through binoculars and the drizzle, none too sure whether they weren't admiring massed rainclouds, harbingers of more bad weather. Equally, he could choose to stroll along the Larchwood Promenade, so smooth and restful in the way it followed the mountainside above the bed of the Reuss. Or else go and see the baker-woman who every evening went through the motions of watering the geraniums in the windowboxes at the *Bäckerei*, a captivating creature who recognised him by now and would acknowledge his smile with a bob of her large round blonde head.

The opening 'fan of possibilities' affords an image, insufficient and misleading though it may be, for Freedom. So maintained the great Hegel (whom I find it diverting to invoke here, precisely because he's so out of place in this little chronicle). As for the Count, all the possible options which seemed to fan out before him there beneath the Dammastock were undoubtedly associated with freedom. But with other things too, for instance his no longer' feeling worn-out, done in and run-down as he habitually did. And now this good feeling of the blood pounding just beneath the skin, throbbing with simple, innocent, youthful impulses. Well, tolerably youthful.

How clean and neat it was, how spick and span that little

railway station lost amid the mighty Alps. Each pane of glass in every door shone like a mirror, which could not always be said for those in the Quirinal Palace. One long plate of glass now mirrored the solid, well-built figure of a man. Forty-ish, or only a little more. A satisfied man, hence sure of himself at last, straight up and down from shoulder to hip. A twinkle in his eye.

Memories of his night in Wassen with the sculptress of ravens, the straddler of mules. (She too rejuvenated as if at the wave of a wand, after he had been made to think of her as elderly, even decrepit.) An adventure concluded rapidly between ten and midnight. But at that happy moment did he not have another option, the freedom to open it up again? He could invite the lady over here, to Goeschenen. What was to stop him? Brighenti, and Gherardesca above all, were out of the way, having had the admirable idea of playing truant. He could telegraph her. Ah, but how does one go about sending a telegram? He had never had to, not once in his entire life. And how should he phrase the invitation, so soon after bidding her goodbye? 'Anxious to return generous hospitality. Affectionately, Moriana.' Or 'most devotedly'? Hang it, La Goltz was no Virgin of the Rocks: 'Your Moriana.' Bit banal. No matter, he was no poet and *'bien à Vous'* is common enough, and sufficiently non-committal.

Settled. The cable (his 'dispatch') was duly compiled and within a few minutes was winging its way along the wires to Wassen and the beautiful (beautiful?) Frau Von Goltz. Which good lady, let it not be forgotten, could very well decline the offer, might just possibly have something better in hand for the morrow. Never mind that, *pazienza*. He wasn't going to let it upset him, he was far too well.

From the telegraph office he strolled out onto the station platform. Outside the Buffet long tables were set, already spread with table-cloths and food to tempt the hearty appetites of travellers who might wish to break their journey. In point of fact a train could be heard approaching, chugging up the steep incline to Goeschenen on the northern track.

But it was a goods train, grey and interminable, at least twenty waggons, too much for two locomotives to haul, so there was a third, a banking-engine helping at the back. When the waggons finally came to a standstill, taking up the entire platform, he walked closer to investigate. Several of the waggons were carrying an interesting load. They were from Belgium and each contained six powerful Friesian draught-horses heavily pawing the straw, hobbled shoulder to shoulder in threes. The great, slow eyes, brimming with distress and submission: so soft, so beautiful. The attendants were giving them hay, and some had got out to fill up wooden pails and water them. The good rich smell of the stable they gave off thrilled him. Like a small boy he wished his pockets were full of sugar-lumps. One of the men informed him the Friesians were on their way to Verona, for the Agricultural Fair. Within ten days those unsold would be crossing Europe again, hauled back through the freezing bowels of the mountains. Our restless modern age, he thought to himself ruefully, which cannot even leave horses in peace, posting them from one end of the Continent to the other.

The smell of the horses mingled with the steam from the engines, and eventually his steps took him down to the rear of the train where men were uncoupling the third engine which would no longer be needed after the long climb to Goeschenen. It was watering-time for the engine too: through a big canvas sleeve thrust into its tank glacier water was flooding from a cistern to quench the thirst of the overheated giant. It kept on puffing heavily, a fitful panting which gave a real sense of fatigue, not simply of power. The thick steel shafts, the connecting rods, were literally sweating, giving off smoke and sizzling with oil. The engine-driver reached out a hand towards the red-painted wheels which were as high as he was, and from the way he did it you could tell the metal must be scorching. So the Machine Age is not simply mechanical. Machines toil and sweat, and thirst, and live. This man who had so often travelled by train began to realise he had never even looked at them until that moment. On a bronze plaque fixed to the boiler he could read its name: '*Sankt Gotthard*' – together with a sort of pedigree: '*Winterthur 1866, Sprüngli und Weber Ingg. Schweizerische Maschinenfabrik.*' So they actually record its date of birth and lineage. Astonishing.

After being uncoupled from the train, the *Sankt Gotthard*, breathing steadily again (only broken-winded animals do not settle down quickly after the race is over) reversed along the track. The driver drove with nonchalant ease using only one hand, his cigarette held in the other, for all the world like an aristocratic horseman with perfect mastery of his mount. He braked at the end of the platform, on the turntable. By operating a lever on the ground he could rotate the whole locomotive, and so there it was a moment later, nose pointing in the opposite direction. The man got down again and went off to down a tankard of beer, but came straight back out and with rag and oil-can set about the job of cleaning and lubricating. Piston-rods, guide-rails, lamps, signal-bell. This attention was in all likelihood quite spontaneous and affectionate, with no sense of obligation or necessity attaching to it.

'Tell me, friend,' the Count inquired, 'what sort of a job is it being an engine-driver?'

The man looked him up and down.

'You get used to it,' he answered presently, in good French.

'It needs a special talent, I expect.'

'You need a delicate touch.'

And he went on to explain that between Erstfeld and Goeschenen there were 25 kilometres of bends over a 35-kilometre stretch, virtually all of them in tunnels.

'I play the violin in my spare time and handling a loco is like playing the fiddle. Coming up I was at the tail. Give it too little steam and we'd be pulled not pushing. Give her too much and the middle waggons can easily jump the rails on a bend. You've got to handle that regulator like the bow of a fiddle. It needs the right touch.'

The Count was only too aware how conversations of this sort are expected to end: with a gift of some kind. A disagreeable custom, humiliating, but impossible not to perform. Any job, not just that of engine-driver, is a matter of habit, a series of repeated actions.

'You smoke cigars, don't you? Take this.'

He mounted the step and handed up the box of Diez Hermanos, the Havanas he had bought in the Buffet.

Well, well, he mused to himself. I'm beginning to acquire a fancy for rolling-stock. It was yet another novel sensation. Machines, machinery factories, machinery exhibitions, had never held any appeal for him.

He set off for the hotel and before he got there he had hit on the answer. Simple enough. Today he was plain *Signor* Filiberto Moriana and so he went along with the March of Progress. 'On duty' it had always been repugnant to him, and with good cause. Kings, if they are consistent, must rightly abhor it as the beginning of their end. The bright noonday sun of Progress is their twilight hour, and all his kind were marching straight into the sunset. And the real enemy? Not Cavallotti, the Radical, or Bissolati, the Socialist: it was anachronism. The notion of a socialist King might be just about conceivable, but he would only serve to highlight his own obsolescence.

We're all of us on the way out, he said to himself, or being pensioned off. In ten years' time, or fifty, the only place for us will be in museums, along with the Anarchists who take pot-shots at us, while sensible people are content to pity us or put us in cartoons, until the day we decide to relegate ourselves to the attic. Up here, I have temporarily resigned my commission, and that's why engines are starting to interest me. I am not a King in civvies, or even on holiday. I've retired. A bit before my time.

He got no further than the hotel forecourt and this conclusion. For him it was already extravagant enough. Reflection, intro- spection, self-analysis? He acknowledged he had certain manias and foibles, but peculiarities of that nature, never. He was for living life as it comes.

Mancuso came to greet him with the news that the steinbock had been found and it now reposed safely in the village ice-house. Vigliotti had volunteered to join the expedition but had been brought back on a stretcher. A real nasty fall, as he was coming down. They'd all carried him up to his room, with a foot this big.

So, once again, he dined alone. And after dinner he repaired to the reading-room which was occupied by only one or two other residents. He started a game of Bishop's solitaire, or Three Clubs, and very soon became utterly, beatifically, engrossed; especially because, strangely enough, this evening it gave every appearance of wanting to 'come out'. It came. Nothing short of a miracle. He'd been having a go at it for months without success. On the stroke of ten he collected his candle from the porter and headed for the stairs, recollecting how in the Quirinal whenever he had to go from one part of the building to another he would be preceded by two flunkeys with candelabra raised aloft at night, and a chamberlain bellowing from room to room: 'The King! The King!' Hideous thought.

On the landing halfway up he met the Mansolin girl coming down. The little blonde creature.

'What a ghastly evening, Count.'

'Ah yes, of course. Your Vigliotti. Now how did it happen? And where are you off to now?'

'I was looking for you, Count. To see if you couldn't cheer me up a bit. I'm so depressed.'

Cheer her up? Rather a liberty, surely.

And yet that candour of hers, so lacking in protocol, it rather pleased him, and the little scene was quite unexpected and really quite charming, here on the narrow panelled landing by the light of their two candles.

Depressed she did not look. With a smile like that?

He escorted her back downstairs, and led her over to the table he had only just left. Drinks were ordered. La Mansolin's eyes were upon him. They seemed to say: Let's see what he makes of me, this famous monster, what will he find to say?

'Having a nice stay then, Signorina?'

That was all. At which she, resuming her plaintive tones:

'Oh, this weather. Rain, rain, and nothing but rain. I've done a few walks. I'm running through some of the classics.'

'Classics?'

'Yes, on the piano. I have a pianoforte diploma. And then there's my fiancé, poor man. But I think he'll get better soon.'

'Of course. One must always look on the bright side.'

Not a very weighty conversation, but they were warming to each other. He escorted her back upstairs, Clara Mansolin and Frau Schwartz's rooms being in the hotel annexe which was joined to the building by a little covered arcade. Deserted. Clara looked out of an open window.

'Snow!'

A little light sleet was falling.

For a minute or two they stood there together with the wind and wet in their faces, and no light since the draught had blown out their candles. She announced that that morning she had been right up the Gotthard Pass, in the diligence. And there was ever such a lot of snow up there, it was quite amazing to see.

'It's a frightful shame the Count was not with us. You see, for me Kings' – she corrected herself, the word did not seem to have a sufficiently regal ring – 'Sovereigns, for me, are like the high mountains. And I think they must feel their very best up among the high mountains.'

Poor child, she didn't know what she was talking about.

'You'll never guess the number of my room. Thirteen! And Frau Schwartz, the lady with me, is right at the other end of the corridor. Number 20. And in the whole of the corridor we're the only two people. It could be quite frightening!'

Acknowledging a curtsy so deep that her knee pressed the floor, with paternal solicitude he handed her back to Frau Schwartz, who at that moment had emerged from her room to go in search of the girl.

The late Baroque façade of the Hotel Adler had two unusual additional features. In the entrance, standing on the top step with arms folded across his chest: Herr Wüntz, sly and benign. Beside the entrance: a blue plaque inscribed in gold letters in three languages beneath the two-headed eagle of Imperial Russia: 'At this hotel, the 1st day of August 1799, Marshal Aleksandr Suwarow halted at the head of his army. He called for a beaker of milk, and in payment presented a coin to the value of five francs.'

The Count, buttoned in his Mackintosh waterproof, was busy reading it for the umpteenth time (he already knew it by heart). And that is how the person he was waiting for knew that he was waiting for her. She wore a plain high-necked travel-suit in mauve, the skirt cut so daringly short that it revealed the tops of her boots, with a hint of pleating at the hips, and at the hem the narrowest flounce of Venetian lace; the tight-fitting matching bodice tapered to a point in front and behind; the sole accessory was a little purse slung troubadour-fashion from her waist-band and bumping against her thigh. In bizarre contrast to such elegant simplicity she sported a horsewoman's diminutive glossy top-hat tilted over one ear and trimmed with a white muslin ribbon trailing to her shoulders.

She also wore a smile, not looking at the Count as she skipped towards him between the puddles, her petticoats hitched high. The handle of her umbrella was pressed tight between her breasts in an attitude of exaggerated caution, very charming and highly provocative.

But his first response was somewhat gruff:

'What's this? On foot?'

And indeed it did seem strange to him, suddenly finding her there and dressed like that.

'I took the mail-coach. Is no one else permitted to travel incognito?'

'Hush. We can be heard.'

Herr Wüntz was only a few steps away. But then, mollified, he broke into a smile too and taking her arm steered her back across the road. They started out along the Larchwood Promenade overlooking the Reuss but almost at once had to turn back, rain was streaming down and there was nothing for it but to go straight in to luncheon. In any case she had announced: 'I only have two hours.'

The Count toyed with his food. He was not hungry.

'Are you not well?' queried La Goltz with a smile in her eyes that belied her concern.

He was decidedly well. His lack of appetite was due to the power of another one. It is a purely physiological reaction found in fleas (male), men, stallions, rats; though no female of any species, and woman least of all, is aware of it or able to feel anything of the sort. Hence it irked him to have to sit forty minutes at table for a meal which only required twenty.

The lady ate normally, and made conversation too. She told him about an old stag, an outcast solitary stag that was causing havoc among the herd on the Meiner Alp above Wassen. Reluctantly she had decided to have it put down by the head game-keeper, all the alps and larch forests in that zone being her property, but now she would be delighted to reserve the stag for the Count's carbine – should he wish to take up the offer. So, before their second tryst had really begun, the lady was angling for a third. This flattering thought reduced, though for no physiological reason, the first appetite to the advantage of the second, and the Count attacked the Emmenthal and Gruyère with relish.

Luncheon over, the fulfilment of one urge prompted the other to reassert itself with renewed vigour which mounted as they ascended the stairs (he planned to conduct La Goltz to the sitting-room on the top floor where they would take coffee together and sit for a moment or two so as not to awaken the suspicions of the staff). Ah, that silk-swathed form climbing the stairs ahead of him, at times lingering strategically to allow for closer inspection of trim calves and soft flanks . . . But then came a sudden dwindling of power just as they were preparing to slip into the safety of the sitting-room. And through no fault of his.

La Goltz remarked, lowering her voice to a whisper:

'The Emperor has written. He is pleased you have chosen Switzerland for your holiday. Where he himself may shortly be coming for a few days.'

'What's that? The Emperor?'

'Yes,' she confirmed, with cool pride.

'Do you mean to say that Wilhelm knows I am here?'

'I took the liberty of informing him.'

'Then you have betrayed my secret!'

His voice was trembling, though the rebuke contained far more dismay than annoyance. A real bitterness.

'Your secret has not been betrayed. No one here knows who you are. And you had good proof of that just now.'

She was alluding to the leisurely fashion in which they had been served at table, just like any other customers, and to his evident impatience.

'As for Wilhelm, if I may say so, he is a colleague and a sincere friend to you.'

Quite, 'a colleague'. Someone, above all, one doesn't tell tales about.

'Good. And now perhaps we should consider ourselves.'

There was no reason to hold back any longer. Time for action. The secrecy which he had so much savoured in anticipation, the stealthy transition from sitting-room to bedroom (ten steps, midway along the corridor, sharp right) lost all its fascination.

She left at four, without allowing him to accompany her to the post-station or even to the bottom of the stairs. He felt disappointed, disgruntled: his 'best time' was later in the day, and preferably after a little break, a bite to eat, a quick cigar. Apart from this, although she could be irritating at times, he was beginning to feel quite taken with the woman. Oh, she irritated him all right. The deliberate gaucherie (calling him *Monsieur l'Comte* when he would have expected *mon copain*, and deserved *mon cochon*), her way of retreating behind enigmatic little bursts of laughter at the most inappropriate moments, and those playful ironic asides ('at our age') and cutting allusions which did not even spare herself ('my old gooseflesh', when she was as dry and smooth as few twenty-year-olds could boast). On the other hand she was also capable of words and actions of an indisputable sincerity — and here he was heeding one of his least fallible instincts — an inventive enthusiasm communicated to her partner through a captivating fund of looks and gestures. At forty-five, was the Count about to be converted to a taste for imaginative love-making, for more sophisticated and demanding feminine extravagances? The truth is that such propensities lay dormant within him, an unfulfilled part of his Habsburg inheritance still to be explored; and La Goltz was a discovery, and a discoverer, for this man who by his own admission felt stale and glutted.

He let her go, and a minute later set out after her. The Gotthard stage was punctual to the second and he arrived only in time to see her boarding it. He called out, but she was not the type to look back.

To cap it all, as he was coming back across the road through the dust kicked up by the horses as they set out for Wassen, he all but tripped over a black cat. And on a Friday of all things, and still only four in the afternoon. His amorous thoughts vanished as quickly as her carriage.

Opposite the post-station was a small road which cut about half an hour off the journey to the Goeschener Alp by the main road. He started out along it, never having explored that way before, but after a few minutes he took a right fork over a wooden bridge spanning the Weissbach, a tributary of the Reuss, and continued on the level alongside the brook. This new road was well-kept and fairly wide, with evidence that heavy loads had been hauled that way, and eventually it opened out into a wide beaten clearing. Sitting down on a stone he picked up a piece of brick lying at his feet and without particularly thinking what he was doing scratched three numbers on the stone: '9–89'. A date, in short, after which he added the initial 'M'. Why? He asked himself the same question. An act of homage (or of remorse) towards his wife; not especially appropriate, it might well be objected, but quite involuntary, and therefore spontaneous.

Some day he would tell her about it. One afternoon up there in Switzerland I inscribed the date on a stone and the first letter of your name. '*Oh toi! tu en as de bien bonnes,*' she would retort. 'No, really I did.'

He raised his eyes and they met a sight which made them blink in amazement. A great wall of rock bounded the clearing in front of him. A section of rock, perhaps three metres by two, had suddenly swung open, along with its stones, its lichen, and its tufts of grass. Behind it yawned a dark cavity.

Yet not so dark that his keen sight failed to make out the muzzle of a huge cannon. A forty-pounder at least. A fortress gun.

The vision only lasted an instant, because the rock-door quickly closed again. With the precision of a bank-vault door. Without a jolt, without a sound.

There was a sound behind him, though, the next moment. Men in uniform, and with bayonets fixed.

'*Was tun Sie hier?*'

Well, the three men were not as startling as what he had witnessed a moment earlier. He began to understand the situation and answered calmly, in French. One of the three, an NCO, shouted back in the same tongue:

'Military Zone. You have no right to be here. And what's that number you wrote on that stone?'

The NCO, having detailed one of his men to go off presumably to obtain instructions as to his next move, proceeded to examine the hapless tourist's passport with a mixture of disdain and deep suspicion. Obviously he had chanced upon one of the many installations which transform the upper reaches of that valley into a fortress, with communication trenches, gun-batteries in caves, barracks and depots buried deep in the mountainside.

Almost a full hour passed (his guards allowed him a smoke) before the officer-in-charge arrived on the scene. A captain. Correct, if none too friendly.

'I am obliged to take your passport particulars. And where are you staying?'

'Do you believe it to be in your hospitable country's interests to treat a foreigner who happens to take a walk as though he were a spy?'

'Take your walks, but refrain from writing dates on stones And pay more attention to what certain notices say.'

He escorted him back to the bridge. Unlike the others it was not made of tree-trunks but well-constructed from solid four-square timbers, and equipped with a large sign which had previously escaped his notice: 'Keep Out'.

A slight misadventure, for an ordinary mortal. But a different matter for him. It did, indubitably, confirm what the beautiful La Goltz had said – 'No one here knows who you are' – but on the other hand it constituted a serious threat to that very incognito, with repercussions that might not be long in coming.

Gherardesca, back from the excursion to Lake Lucerne, was waiting for him on the steps of the Adler. He asked whether there was anything new to report or any orders. Should he tell him about the encounter in the Goeschener Alp? He decided to keep it under his hat, hoping that the Armed Forces of the Swiss Confederation would continue to remain in ignorance of what an eminent (and innocuous) prisoner they had had at their mercy.

VI

———————— • ————————

Dr Brighenti took great pains over his dressing, completing the operation by rubbing a little Eau de Felsina into his beard. The chambermaid had called to let him know that Fräulein Mansolin and Frau Schwartz were unwell and would appreciate a visit.

He tried the Fräulein first.

'The doctor in Padua says I suffer from "stygmatic hysteria", but I've never understood what he means . . .'

'Out of the question.'

'But, doctor, I have the most frightful nerves! Up here in the mountains I haven't slept the past three nights.'

'Valerian. Valerian.'

'And this morning I just don't seem to have the strength to get up. I'm dog-tired, honestly. Besides – come a bit closer, Professor – I have a little confession to make.'

That rosebud just peeping out of the little lace mantilla with the pink ribbons – it was a pleasure to come closer. He sat on the edge of her bed and felt for her pulse.

'No, no. What's that for? I have to confess something. But can I say it in French?'

'Just use Italian.'

'No! In French. *C'est depuis quelques mois que . . . que j'ai repris mes habitudes de collégienne.*'

'My dear child. Calm yourself. We must not exaggerate. Does it happen often?'

'*Cela dépend.* It depends on the opportunities I have.'

'But seeing the bridegroom exists, why don't you hurry up and get married?'

'Next month. Don't go yet, I have another confession. Can you guess? I don't love him.'

'Don't love him? Why ever not?'

'I just don't! Do you promise not to tell anyone?'

'I'm offended. Professional secrecy, you know. But I must say I'm a bit surprised. That Vigliotti. A fine-looking fellow, and destined to go far.'

'I know. He's rich and he'll go far, that's why I'm marrying him. But there's someone I can't get out of my head. Somebody who proposed to me two or three years ago. We only ever met in the street and I'm so short-sighted I never even managed to see if he was handsome or ugly. He was well-dressed, and intelligent too, and he had a beautiful voice. He spoke about love in such a very sweet way.'

'So why didn't you settle for that one?'

'No money. Also he had an idiotic surname. I had to tell him to leave me alone. A year ago my nerves were in an awful state, I thought of doing myself in. Imagine.'

'Tut tut. Do you mean it?'

'Of course I do. Frau Schwartz dyes her hair black. Honestly, at forty-nine! Well, I knew that the hair-dye she uses is . . . is . . .'

'Pyrogallol.'

'That's right, poison. Anyway one day I go and steal the bottle, and I take a really big gulp . . .'

She laughed, pressing her little head back into the pillows, a laugh which lit up the whole room like a sudden burst of sunshine, on that grey morning.

'I spat it out quick. God, did it taste foul! So you see, Professor, I'm really quite lucky to be here. So what kind of medicines are you going to prescribe for me? No more anti-hysteria water, I hope?'

'I prescribe: plenty of exercise, as much as you can get. Sleep on a hard mattress. Bring forward the wedding-day. Your Vigliotti is the right remedy for you. Fine specimen of a young man. And you'll soon get to love him, mark my words. And now I think I had better be calling on your lady-companion.'

'And I'll go up and see my fiancé. Is it true his foot's fractured?'

'Out of the question. Later on, I promise, I'll look in again to see how you are. And you, my dear, put all ideas of hysteria right out of your mind. That's not a complaint, it's a libel invented by some sick misogynist.'

At number 20 a less poetic spectacle awaited him. More down-to-earth, not to say promising. She too was feeling indisposed, the forty-nine-year-old Frau Schwartz. The widow of an actor who had neglected and betrayed her till his dying day, she sought solace with a pathetic eagerness, transparently visible beneath the matronly decorum and restraints of Helvetian propriety. An eagerness as thinly veiled as the florid forms under the *peignoir* she wore in bed.

She complained of hot flushes on the chest, a cold in the head, and pains in the back.

'Ach, it's the awful greyness of these days. *Der Weltschmerz.* The sorrow of this useless life of ours . . . I know the Herr Professor understands German. May I speak German?'

'Just speak Italian, if you don't mind. I have to uncover you, Signora. May I?'

A pair of shoulders emerged which would have been the envy of a wrestler, but for the fact that they were extraordinarily smooth and white. Brighenti pursed his lips, listening through his stethoscope. Then:

'Uncover yourself in front. Thank you.'

Hippocrates was for excommunicating the physician who mingles profane intentions with the sacred art of healing. Yet surely Hippocrates would have made an exception for patients like the pining Frau Schwartz.

'Oh, Professor,' she kept sighing. 'I feel so peculiar.'

But he: 'Deep breath,' 'Cough,' 'Relax . . .' Outwardly the examination was irreproachable, never an immodest glance or word. His hands sufficed. And that beard redolent of Eau de Felsina, going up and down, softly, smoothly, stealthily.

Outside the hotel coach-house some ten men were waiting: beaters, porters, and a guide, alongside Mancuso and Gherardesca. The plan was to go up to the reserve where they had found the steinbock, but higher still. Steinbock and chamois had been sighted at around two thousand metres during a break in the clouds the day before.

But today nothing could be seen up there, the weather was truly prohibitive. When the Count came down at 8 a.m. they debated the situation. He was for going at all costs, the guide was for deferring the expedition. Gherardesca agreed, apprehensive after Vigliotti's accident. After ten o'clock when there was still no hope of the weather improving those in favour of postponement won the day; when coffee and cognac had been dispensed the party broke up and went its several ways. Gherardesca ventured as far as the post-station and came back with a suggestion. The regular Gotthard diligence had already gone but the coach-master had offered to lay on a supplementary carriage. If the Count was agreeable, why not take a trip to the top of the pass?

Into the five-horse carriage with capacity for twelve climbed the Count, his two aides, and Signorina Mansolin. The thought-ful idea of inviting her along had come from Brighenti. Up visiting Vigliotti in his room (only a strained tendon, no fracture, three days' rest) he had taken pity on little Clara shut in there looking rather grumpy and down in the dumps. Poor soul, a good breath of fresh air was what she needed, his prescription for her was to get out and about. The Count of course was consulted, and was not opposed. At the last moment, again with his leave, they were joined by Frau Schwartz and an acquaintance of hers from Zürich, also staying at the Adler, a reasonably young and nice-looking woman who spoke Italian.

The weather, impossible for hunting, was hardly ideal for an excursion. As far as Andermatt they saw nothing but fog and the black forms of fir-trees fading slowly into the fog. Signorina Mansolin, well-wrapped in scarves and plaids, had clambered onto the top of the carriage to install herself on the imperial, the baggage platform behind the postilion, and could be heard uttering cries of enthusiasm in her shrill tuneless voice. What she found to thrill her so much was beyond the Count's comprehen-sion, but she sounded happy. With him inside the carriage, Gherardesca was snoozing, every so often waking with a start to screw his monocle back in his eye, and Brighenti intensified his furtive advances towards Frau Schwartz seated opposite him. The Count turned to Frau Tschudi, the lady from Zürich who was a teacher of Italian in a high-school, and asked her a question every now and again.

'Is the Italian colony in Zürich very large?'

Right now – he mused – that Captain could be compiling his report. 'Foreign presence detected in locality such-and-such, Goeschenen Military Zone.' Tomorrow it will be on the Area Commander's desk, and he will forward it to Counter-Espionage as their responsibility. And then Counter-Espionage will request information from the Italian authorities. 'Person answering to the name of Filiberto Di Moriana . . .' No, what nonsense. Who would ever dream of seeking information from the authorities of a country where the presumed spy comes from? They conduct on-the-spot enquiries. What he is doing here, who he has dealings with. In his case: La Goltz. Foreign herself, and German into the bargain. Germans are not too popular round here, not after what happened back in '70. In 1870 a Bavarian army had actually contemplated violating Helvetian virginity.

'Do you have a great many students on your Italian course?'

Come, come. La Goltz is so well-known here, a lot of people owe a living to her, she's rich. It's common knowledge that she's the widow of a Krupp. Such prominent people are not recruited as spies.

He settled back in his corner and did not speak again. Preoccupied. His palms were a little sweaty, his forehead too, and he felt a certain difficulty in getting his breath. The altitude?

Hardly. The altitude could not be to blame. He had toiled up and down mountains, from the Fréjus to the Tonale, a hundred times without ever suffering the least adverse effect. No, it was rather that the long evening shadows were beginning to close in upon him, the climacteric. The gradual and inexorable 'withdrawal from active service'. Who was it now (his father?) who used to say that a man is fit to live only as long as he excites women and scares men?

The only men he scared now were the frontier guards. Or they scared him. Mind, there was always a chance that Captain's report would never go off. Send in a report and next thing you have an inspection, an investigation, and whoever sets his signature to it is the first to take the rap. Lax security etc. Very true. Even so, there was no reason to take much comfort from it.

At the very top, in the desolate solitude of the pass, they encountered a wan sun and (curious at over two thousand metres) a tepid sirocco wind blowing from the South. The Count's mood did not improve. They pulled up at the inn, the sole sign of human habitation apart from a pair of pine-log huts in all that silent expanse, and when the time came to take their seats at table he found a pretext for eating alone, and ate little.

It was Clara, after lunch, who got him out of his corner.

'Can I ask you something, Count?'

'Fire away.'

'Would you keep me company?'

Just like that, bold as brass.

'Where?'

All the same he followed her out. From the inn a track led straight up the mountain, and in a moment they were alone among huge, smooth, black boulders, in shapes as primordial as the basalt they were made of. The girl made one or two half-hearted attempts to break the silence before the wilderness overwhelmed her, became too intimidating.

'If you weren't with me I'd die of fright.'

He took her arm.

'But would you mind telling me why it was me you turned to?'

Then came this astonishing reply:

'Because the others are all old.'

Well, that woman from Zürich, Frau Tschudi, could be at most thirty-five, and even Gherardesca was only forty, five years younger than himself, whether or not he looked it. And yet her reply had been so immediate, so serious, so unhesitating, that he felt it impossible to question its spontaneity. His step became brisker, his breathing steadier despite the climb. He ought to have demurred, made a mocking reference to his greying temples, but did not take the trouble. After all, why not accept the little present?

'I'm so sorry,' little Goldilocks resumed after a pause, 'to see you look sad.'

Again he was wise enough not to reply.

'Still, sadness suits your features. The Count's face is made for deep things.'

Laugh? He would not have dreamed of doing so. Of all the women who had paid court to him, she was the only one who had managed it with such tact and charm. That she was paying court was only too plain by now. And if she really was sincere? What if she really had noticed that he was not an expansive man nor an optimist, and had never had any reason to be?

'How beautiful she was, that lady you had with you.'

'What lady?'

'The lady who had lunch with you yesterday.'

At this he could not suppress a smile. A little hint of jealousy, and moreover so gracefully revealed. This Mansolin girl really was a capital little lady. Her efforts should not go unrewarded.

'Tell me, why did you go and hide yourself away up on the imperial? And in this weather.'

No very plausible explanation was offered, and in any case it did not matter to the Count. They had reached an understanding, nothing more needed to be said. They turned back. He led the way, head held high, glad to fill his lungs with the good mountain air, and every now and again, where the path was a little tricky to negotiate, turning round to offer her his hand.

Still, she had quite a mind of her own, the little blonde-haired thing. When it was time to leave she clambered straight back up to her favourite perch under the hood, and stayed up there until they arrived. The Count, inside the carriage, was left to endure Brighenti's booming Bolognese voice and the soft snoring of Gherardesca, asleep with his hands clasped under his paunch.

At Andermatt, where they halted for a coffee, Brighenti returned from the Hotel Bellevue, the largest in Canton Uri and the most frequented, to report that the Chef was from Bologna like himself. He vowed he would come back next day for a good plate of tagliatelle as a break from the grisly Swiss fodder, and La

Schwartz and La Tschudi, who had no particularly strong patriotic feelings about the 'fodder', immediately volunteered to join him. It was agreed to book the same relief vehicle on the St Gotthard line, departure at noon, seeing it was a journey of only a few kilometres. The Count gave his authorisation, but left his own options open.

Next morning La Mansolin said she could not leave her fiancé. But at midday she seemed to think she had martyred herself long enough, and she joined the band. In the end the Count thought he might just as well come along too, and so the coach set out with the same party as before, tunnelling through the same fog. When they all got down at Andermatt (La Mansolin from her look-out post on the imperial: the cold air put such colour back in her cheeks) the Count, who had not yet seen the big hotel from close to, was assailed by doubts. He resolved to conduct a personal reconnaissance. He was back out in a flash. He had asked to be shown the register of guests, and among them appeared no less a figure than Von Lichnowsky, the Austro-Hungarian Foreign Minister.

Consternation!

'You go ahead by all means. But count me out,' said the Count.

'How could we desert you, we are under your orders . . .'

'I order you to go in. And you, Brighenti, shame on you for the greedy hog you are. For shame!'

Nowhere could the Professor find his handkerchief to mop the beads of perspiration from his brow.

The Count's temper soon simmered down, and truth to tell he passed two very agreeable hours, utterly free and alone. He walked through the village which was thronged with trippers and on through fields where they were gathering the last of the August hay, above him a leaden sky at whose fringes everyone vainly sought the famous silhouettes of the Mutthorn and the Finsteraarhorn, immortalised by Baedeker and by every postcard on sale. Their non-appearance was of no account to the Count. Regaining the village he went into the first *Gasthaus* and had a meal, washing it down with several tankards of garnet-coloured beer of excellent quality.

Opposite him at the same table were two men in Tyrolean

jackets but speaking French, while at his left elbow was an old man of the mountains with a face as red as a strawberry who having satisfied his appetite and slaked his thirst folded his arms across the tablecloth, sank his head upon them and quietly nodded off. The French (or French-Swiss, or Belgians) were bandying impressions of Italy, whence they had apparently just arrived. They had been struck by the sheer scale of everything in Italy. The variety of police-forces (three of them, rivals yet not competitors, even four according to some calculations), the number of killings (Italians murder each other without cease, and preferably without motive), the hordes of unemployed day-labourers in village squares, the immense and unremitting uproar thanks to which the foreign visitor in Florence, in Genoa, in Milan, might just as well not waste his time trying to grab any sleep, day or night. The prodigious quantity of litter and empty bottles enhancing the natural beauty of the landscape, on the beaches, in the fields, all over the hills. Further peculiarities: if a train arrives at a station less than twenty minutes behind sched-ule, if a letter reaches its destination within three days of being posted, all who are party to the miracle cross themselves 'just like we do when a calf is born with two heads'.

Thus was he comforted by the latest news of his happy Realm. All the same, due to the effects of the beer he was beginning to feel rather drowsy and envied his neighbour to the left who was sleeping so soundly through it all. Without much hope of success he adopted the same position, and shut his eyes.

Miraculous: he dropped off. And slept a good half hour. He made their rendezvous, fixed at a suitable distance from the perilous Hotel Bellevue, an equal number of minutes late. Only the ladies were at the carriage: Brighenti and Gherardesca were toiling up and down the streets of Andermatt looking for him. Serve them right. Just what the doctor ordered for that hog Brighenti, and that other sluggard.

All present and correct, they set off at last. La Mansolin had finally deserted her post on the imperial (and just as well for her, as we shall see) and was installed opposite him, inside the carriage. A timid little foot slipped between his own, with the humble insistence of an entreaty for forgiveness. What did the little thing have to apologise for? Their separation, which had lasted the whole of the day? It might be.

On their way back they saw the sun again. A new-born, prodigal sun which through the clouds and between each fir-tree-top sent spurts of gold, blackening the shadows; a sun still high enough to set the glaciers alight, the summits wheeling with every twist and turn of the road. La Mansolin put her head out of the window (without removing her foot).

'Gosh, now it's so beautiful,' she whispered. 'Isn't it now?'

They were moving too fast for serious appreciation of the scenery. The postilion must have set his mind on making up for lost time, and he plied his whip.

The St Gotthard diligence, with its postilions, its select horses, its post-horn, its colours of yellow and blue, did not fail to live up to the legend which the literature of half of Europe (from England to Germany and Russia) had created round it. It was both a commodious and an adventurous mode of transportation. Punctual in the best Swiss tradition, but moving at a spanking pace and a real bully on the road: woe to anyone who would not give way. The one which the Count and his company had hired was no different to the regular mail-coach, it had the same privileges of the highway and could allow itself an even greater velocity.

On the descent to Goeschenen the driver displayed all his skill, and the Count who was a connoisseur of such things, being himself an expert handler of four-horse teams, was lost in admiration. The style with which they skimmed past the roadside posts was perfect. The powerful hindquarters of the front two horses, the steerage pair, served where necessary to reduce the heavy vehicle's speed, as well as the brakes of course.

They flew over the famous Teufelbrücke, the Devil's Bridge, at top speed. Immediately afterwards came a series of fairly tight bends. The coachman checked his steeds, and resolutely applied the brakes.

The brake-blocks, for the umpteenth time, clamped into the iron wheel-hoops. Just as they were about to swing into the last bend (the roofs of Goeschenen heaving in sight) a nail sprang loose; split in two, the big hoop spun into the air and landed behind squirming in the dust like a snake, leaving the brake-shoe free to bite deep into the stout oak wheel, which held for an instant or two. Then it gave way and broke into pieces, the spokes shooting off one after the other at a tangent like bolts from a cross-bow. The sound was an excellent imitation of a burst of machine-gun fire. The carriage swayed, tipped, toppled over to the right. Far beneath them, at the foot of the ravine, roared the foaming white waters of the Tiesbach, as they tumbled towards the Reuss.

PART TWO
A COUPLE ON DETACHMENT

VII

───────────── • ─────────────

Interlude in heaven (heaven of the Spirit, or Idea). Seated on her throne, the terraqueous globe at her feet, History must decide the ultimate fate of one of her Dramatis Personae. She is in two minds, scratches her periwig. Now, or in a lustrum or two? This coach, or another?

The fate of the remaining half dozen men and women in the party is of no concern to her. They are men and women, precisely, and *de parvis humani generis non curat Historia*. In the midst of her deliberations Chance steps in, unbidden. An irrepressible intruder, as Professor Hegel was compelled to recognise after racking his brains for a way to get rid of her. And Chance decides, all alone.

As chance would have it, then, the driver of the carriage, Hans Seiler by name, domiciled at Hospenthal, had reduced speed moments earlier having caught sight of a trap on which were travelling, seated behind their driver, two mendicant Franciscan nuns, one of whom happened to be Hans Seiler's wife's first cousin. Chance further decreed that the road which at that point ran sheer above the Tiesbach should be protected, because of a recent landslip, by a temporary wooden parapet—not a particularly strong one, but stout enough to provide support and smooth enough not to snag. It was no more than twenty yards in length: the imperial, without baggage or passengers on it, scraped along the top of the parapet while the wheel-stump ploughed a furrow beneath it, bringing the vehicle to a standstill little more than a hand's breadth or two from the point where the parapet ended and the abyss yawned.

Seiler, unhurt, ran forward to hold back the terrified horses. The left-hand door of the diligence opened and onto the road dropped (about five feet due to the tilt of the coach) one of the passengers. Gherardesca. After him piled out, likewise un-scathed, Brighenti and the Count.

Together the three men grasped the side of the diligence and managed to right it with one heave. Then they bodily hauled out La Schwartz and La Tschudi – bodily because both had passed out in the approved fashion. Finally they gave Clara a leg down. Not only was she in full possession of her faculties, she looked more rosy-cheeked than ever and quite unperturbed. Declining the proffered brandy flask she dug a bar of chocolate out of Frau Schwartz's travel-bag, and started to nibble.

They were only a kilometre short of the village. So when the ladies had recovered from their fright the Count urged them all to start walking.

'On you go. I'll stay here to give this good fellow a hand.'

Chorus of ceremonious protestations.

'No, no, I must insist.'

The little band vanished into the mouth of the tunnel which began a few paces further down the road, Brighenti bringing up the rear so that he could peer at a bump contracted in a spot which could not very well be inspected in front of the ladies. The Count went over to the horses which Seiler had hitched up in order to have his hands free to sort out the tangle of reins and traces. In these matters the Count possessed a genuine compe-tence, one of his few, and it was only natural that he should take pleasure in exercising it, while also assisting one of his fellow-creatures. Unfortunately horses, even the best-bred among them, can be 'temperamental' at times. In other words they bite. The one which bit the Count could chew hard enough to cut right through his glove. Drawing blood.

Clara, contrary to instructions, had been waiting in the shadow of the tunnel entrance. She ran to him.

'He's been assassinated!'

The Count snickered.

'Not yet.'

He was a little hard of hearing; a consequence, perhaps, of his martial exploits, the guns of Villafranca and all that. All she had said was simply: 'It's bleeding, isn't it?' In no time the little thing had plucked his handkerchief out of his breast pocket, dowsed it in some Eau de Cologne she kept in her handbag and wrapped it round the wound.

'And now do come along. You really must!'

And as they set out to follow the others the girl added:

'You shouldn't expose yourself to such risks. You are too important.'

'Too important' – this time he had heard her perfectly, and yet not for one moment did he suspect that it was a cry of devotion to the monarchy. (And after all was not this the same man who long years before had entrusted this selfless thought to the privacy of his diary: 'What do I want with *la monarchia*, long live *la mona*'? – the last of the attributes peculiar to womankind in his little maxim which we cited in chapter III.) In the first few moments the facts seemed to bear out the interpretation he put on them: they entered the tunnel, and stooping forward to meet the darkness he encountered, moist and meekly parted, two fresh young lips. Unresisting.

'I'm not going to get another scolding?' were her first words.

Extraordinary.

'Scolding?'

'You see, two years ago I did my school-leaving exams and when we had the Latin unseen I hid a grammar down my front. Nobody saw me get it out, except you. You were watching me.'

'I was?'

'Yes. Your portrait over the teacher's desk. And you looked so severe. You were ticking me off.'

That same Sunday afternoon a quite different travel mishap had concluded no less felicitously in the vicinity of Goeschenen railway station. Only a minute after the Milan–Zürich express had left for Erstfeld.

There exists a Swiss organisation known as the 'Samaritans', non-denominational though Calvinist in origin, and renowned throughout the Confederation for the physical strength of its followers and their evangelical energy. One of its members was a Goeschenen cowherd by the name of Peter Weiss. That afternoon Peter and his horse and cart were on their way to the village to deliver some milk when on the path, which at one point runs alongside the railway embankment, he came upon the figure of a gentleman sitting on the ground. A pained grimace distorted his features, and he was rubbing an ankle. At the sight of Peter he endeavoured to twist the grimace into a smile and called out to him, in German: 'I fell off the train.'

Peter wasted no words. Picking up the poor man he dumped him among the urns on the back of his cart and put his horse to a trot. After a stop at the grocery-cum-pharmacy which refused to open its doors (it was a Sunday) he reined up before the Adler, where he offloaded a portion of the milk and helped the sufferer up the flight of steps. On the top step Herr Wüntz, proprietor, looked round to check the porter was at his post, but otherwise did not turn a hair. Mission accomplished, the good Peter proceeded on his way cheerily refusing all offers of remuneration or even gratitude, according to the time-honoured code of all good Samaritans.

The gentleman, caked in mud to the tips of his ears, inquired whether a room might be available. One might. The porter, unused to receiving people in such poor shape, coatless, hatless, and minus luggage, first requested he enter his name, surname, and place of residence in the register – clearly, please. This presented no problems. On the counter in the Bureau stood a pot containing the Swiss national flag around which those of four or five other European countries were grouped, to denote the provenance of the hotel's various residents. Conspicuous by its absence was the Union Jack. Fine, the newcomer would make good the omission. In the register he printed: '*Walter Fairtales, Businessman, London*'.

'The gentleman is without luggage?'

'My bags are still on the train.'

'We could recover them.'

'Then will you be so good as to get the station-master to telegraph? They should be sent here.'

He collapsed into an easy-chair and ordered a strong black coffee.

Now this Mr Fairtales was not so 'absent-minded', as the English say, as to have simply forgotten his baggage in his compartment on the train. Something rather more alarming had befallen him. He had got down at Goeschenen to procure some refreshment and the papers, and had taken a little too long over it. Not that he had failed to catch the train again. By racing after it along the platform he had just managed to grab hold of the doorhandle of the very last coach.

There, balanced on the footboard, he had wrestled to get the door open. Until, to his utter horror, he noticed that the locked and deserted coach was in fact a baggage-van. There was little to be gained by continuing to beat his fist to a pulp on the glass. Either he had to resign himself to hanging on there a good hour or more, since no stops were scheduled before Erstfeld, or else he had to detrain forthwith. He had opted for this latter course of action, calculating that even for a man of thirty-three a jump like that would not be suicidal provided you were lightly built and game for anything. And soft meadow grass was waiting to receive him. Damage was limited to a rough landing, a few scratches and the sprained ankle.

Eventually he managed to negotiate the stairs to his bedroom on the second floor, and at the appointed hour had dinner brought up to him. Next morning his foot was already much improved and on taking his first step outside the room he found his luggage waiting for him. Oh, impeccable Helvetian efficiency! Only 1.50 francs extra was owing to the Federal Railways.

At ten in the morning the lobby of the Hotel Adler was always deserted.

He asked to see the railway timetable and found that he could continue his journey by the same 3 p.m. train from which he had alighted in such unorthodox fashion the day before. In any case he was in no particular hurry, seeing that he was on holiday and his Gretchen (Margaretha Loewenthal, a twenty-eight-year-old bank-clerk from Bavaria, the current girl-friend) would not be arriving in Küsnacht, on Lake Lucerne, before Thursday.

To pass the time he began idly turning the pages of the hotel register. Present residents included Germans, Austrians, French. Also a party of four men from Italy: Vigliotti, Brighenti, Gherardini, Moriana. With one woman: Clara Mansolin, from Padua. Clara?

No use hoping it could be someone else with the identical name. After two years he was about to see once more the only woman who had appealed to him strongly enough to make him imagine there could be no more delicious and desirable fate than to renounce his independence for ever. He had met her in the street one afternoon when he was on a day out in Padua. He had been living in the Veneto at the time. For him, it was love at first sight, the classic *coup de foudre*. For her, as he was in time informed by an eminent lawyer, the sole friend they had in common and her only possible messenger, the answer was no. It appeared that she was already engaged to a certain Gigi, surnamed Chierigo, a name which in the Vento is synonymous with millionaire, being a family of great landowners – and this despite the fact that she was very well-off herself. Fairtales did not give in. He started writing to her again, trailed her about the city. Then one day, in a pastry-shop, politely but very firmly he heard himself informed: 'I should be obliged, Sir, if you would kindly leave me alone.' It is said that thunderbolts, unless they kill, leave no trace. Not so. Fairtales had spent six months licking his wounds.

Clara it was. A little plump, but still with those lovely eyes, so short-sighted and childlike, and that marvellous ash-blonde hair. She was seated in the dining-room not ten feet from his table (without, needless to say, having recognised him), eating and chatting away to a woman of solid Swiss appearance who was with her. A lady companion, no doubt.

In filed a party of four men, all unmistakably Italian, the last pausing to greet Clara. A man of good height, reasonably young, very correct in every detail, to the point of rigidity. Poles apart from Gigi Chierigo. He exchanged a few words in an undertone with Clara, and Fairtales immediately put two and two together: fiancés, not far off the marriage-day. Marriage for money.

The couple's manner with each other had something distinctly conventional about it, even slightly irritable, nothing remotely resembling the gay complicity of two people in love. 'Enjoy your meal, dear,' was all he heard her say, no poetry or passion there. The man, so ultra-correct in every way, leaning on a stick, went off to a table at the other end of the room to rejoin his companions.

One of these was quite clearly superior in rank to the others, all of whom treated him with deference. Fairtales immediately dubbed him 'Signor X'. The moment Signor X finished his meal he rose from table, cigar and a glass of port in his left hand, and made his way towards the next room, the smoking-room. He seemed quite elderly and yet his stride was jaunty, almost cocksure, and his face bore an expression which considerably intrigued Mr Fairtales: it was at once both amused and somewhat abstracted, as if he were smiling at some thought of his own. At table Signor X had not opened his mouth except for the purpose of eating, and speedily at that; not one word had he exchanged with his three table-companions. A taciturn and inattentive man, savouring something to come or else relishing its memory.

A minute or two later Clara Mansolin and her lady companion rose to leave. Fairtales took a last sip of wine, lit up a cigarette, and in his turn went into the neighbouring room, where there were quite a few other people already, for the most part German and Swiss. Clara's chaperone, perched on the edge of a divan, was demurely turning the pages of a magazine. Leaning with his back against the mantelpiece, smoking in silence: Signor X. In a low armchair, her legs crossed: Clara. Right in front of him, eyes fastened on him.

Gripped by a pang of untimely jealousy, Fairtales retreated to the lobby again, and tried to reflect. He asked himself how it could be that four men (Italians, no less) were travelling (or holidaying here) for pleasure without women for company. True, one had his fiancée with him. But relegated to another table, with the entire room between. Second point: what possible amusement could those three men derive from going on holiday with their employer and still patently under his orders? Third: what need could he have, this boss on holiday, for the services of no less than three members of his staff? As for the fact that the betrothed of one of his dependants was flirting with him – well, there was nothing so strange about that. These things happen all the time, the whole world over.

He remembered the names: Vigliotti, Brighenti, Gherardini, etc. But he was not able to fit the names to the faces. He succeeded later in the evening (but only up to a point) in the case of one of them. He had gone out into the driveway in front of the hotel, to get a breath of air. Walking just ahead of him and chatting together he saw the oldest of the Italians, the one with the little grey beard and the bald one with the pot belly, a Florentine to judge by his accent. The first suddenly said loudly: 'Are you going to explain it to me then, Gherardesca, this whole business of the mortgage?' And a moment later, evidently not satisfied: 'No, Gherardesca, these are . . .'

'Fancy that,' thought Fairtales – who appears to be rather an observant character, as well as very well-informed about Italy and things Italian. 'Here we have a Gherardini who then becomes Gherardesca to his associates.'

Now whereas Gherardini was a surname of no consequence, Gherardesca, as he well knew, was a very illustrious name indeed in Italy. Not only for Dante scholars. Also for any friend of the turf, whose number included Mr Fairtales. Gherardesca, or rather Della Gherardesca – Count Brando Della Gherardesca – was a leading authority on matters equestrian, having for many years been President of the Association for the Propagation of the Equine Race, or APER, which controlled all the race-tracks in the Peninsula, from San Siro to L'Arcoveggio and Le Capannelle. He did not know him by sight, but he knew him very well by reputation.

He decided to do a little investigating, and next morning had a real stroke of luck. He looked out of his bedroom window and there, directly below him, was the very same gentleman taking coffee at a little table. On the table was a small pile of magazines, all with the identical cover. None other than the APER Bulletin, which he had no difficulty in recognising. He received it himself, being a subscriber. A big point in favour of Gherardesca, and against Gherardini.

He could do a double-check. He looked through his wallet and fished out his APER personal membership card on which the President's signature was reproduced. Downstairs, he opened the hotel register and compared the two. Instead of 'Brando' an innocuous 'Bernardo'. And yet the two signatures were very similar, even identical, at least in the first part of the surname: 'Gherard'. The same capital G, the same heavy cross-stroke. On the membership card the final 'esca' was little more than a vague squiggle, in the register book the final 'ini' was instead written with precision, with decision. That is, it looked contrived, too deliberate.

Nearly there! Now all he had to do was think up a way of obtaining the proof that clinched it.

Towards midday he secreted himself in a corner of the lobby to wait for the residents to return for lunch. And in came his man. Carefully he watched where he hung up his stick and hat. After the second bell, when all guests and serving-people had gone into the dining-room, he leapt for the hat and took a quick look inside. As he had imagined: inscribed on the maroquin sweat-band were three initials. BDG.

That Brando Della Gherardesca, while travelling abroad for his own pleasure in a country where passports are not compulsory, should amuse himself by changing his name was, all things considered, not particularly remarkable. However, Gherardesca was not abroad alone but in the company of five or six other people, if one counted Clara Mansolin and chaperone. All of them consenting to the subterfuge and if necessary prepared, even concerned, to corroborate the fiction. Were they all collaborating in a practical joke? Fairtales gave it long consideration while he consumed his meal, and finally reached the conclusion that it did not look plausible. In which case their collaboration was of a different kind. It smacked of complicity.

A big smuggling racket? Absolutely not, impossible. And espionage had to be ruled out too. 'BDG' was too well-known a figure. High-level politics, then, international intrigue. Could he be here in Switzerland, neutral territory, on a special mission, expecting the minister of a foreign power, some plenipotentiary, for a secret meeting? More like it. On the other hand it had never come to his ears that 'BDG' had any interest in politics. Neither did it explain his blatant deference towards Signor X, or Signor Moriana – 'the Count', as they all addressed him. A simple pretence to put people off the scent, divert attention? Odd. Whatever the game, Signor X was no mere pawn. If a mission was the answer, then there was no question who was its leader.

Fairtales was really beginning to get his teeth into it. As soon as coffee had been served he went over to the telegraph office and sent off a telegram to a friend in Rome, a journalist, asking him to telegraph back with everything he could find out about the 'present position' of Count Della Gherardesca, the APER President. He also sent a telegram to Margaretha. 'Detained Goeschenen on a job. Letter follows. Love and kisses.' When he returned to the Adler he gave notice that he intended staying three more days.

But at this point in our tale a word of explanation is called for. It is high time, shall we say, to lift the veil obscuring yet another mystery. One which concerns, and conceals, none other than the person of Mr Fairtales himself.

For this gentleman, whom we have observed intruding upon this covert courtly-cum-holiday intrigue set within the solid walls of the Hotel Adler (already touched by Suwarow's martial glory) in those first days of September 1889, was himself a bit of a mystery character, someone with something to hide. Yes, he had his own contribution to make to that atmosphere of uncertainty and intrigue. In the first place he was not 'Fairtales' at all, the name being simply a pseudonym which he had resorted to in the past when submitting for publication certain literary efforts alongside which his true name, Walter Schiapin, would have appeared a little uncouth. Secondly, his native city was not the great metropolis of London but the rather more modest township of Thiene in the province of Vicenza, Italy. He was Italian, therefore, though by blood only half Italian, having been born of a genuine Englishwoman (to whom he owed his command of the language and the resolute empiricism of his outlook). Finally, he had nothing whatsoever to do with the world of commerce. He was a journalist by profession, and a successful one at that who, only a few months earlier, had been promoted to head of the Foreign Desk on a Rome newspaper of a Radical persuasion.

One more figure travelling incognito, then, although in his case it truly was the result of a whim, a flamboyant reaction to his tumble from the train, or to revenge himself upon the suspicious porter. Or even, just possibly, it should be put down to the promptings of that professional sixth sense which every true-born journalist, such as Schiapin, claims to possess in rare moments of inspiration.

In any case Walter Schiapin now intended to treat himself to a couple of days' rest, or as long as it took his colleague in Rome to reply. He put Gherardesca-Gherardini from his mind, and managed not to occupy his thoughts, beyond the strictly inevitable, with the pitiless Clara Mansolin. He still did not feel up to walking very far. Instead of the mule which he asked for they managed to fix him up with a passable pony, suitably saddled, on which he made a couple of sorties. On the second of these he set out along the main road in the direction of the valley, and once through the village he let the animal, of its own accord, turn aside along a path which cut down through the woods.

His mount was no race-horse but over difficult terrain it was as fearless and sure-footed as a goat, and in twenty minutes the steep short-cut had taken them down to Wassen. Not quite to the village itself, for they came out in the neighbourhood of a large and very well-maintained timber lodge of recent construction, which he took to be a hotel. Dismounting, he went in search of someone who could direct him back to the carriage-road. Luck, most decidedly, was on his side. From a clump of pines stepped a lady, very pretty into the bargain, dressed in jodhpurs and riding boots. 'No, it is not a hotel, this is the Von Goltz private residence, but you have permission to cross the land. Keep bearing left and you'll come out on the main road.'

Most interesting. And to ascertain more thoroughly the qualities of Frau Von Goltz (to identify her as such did not demand any great powers of insight) Schiapin switched from German to English.

'Would you be good enough to show me the way across your property?'

'*To my regret, I cannot right now. I'm busy here.*'

And she dived back into the pines.

Excellent English pronunciation, therefore a lady who moved in international circles. Very wealthy too. And equipped with a most unusual personality, as was proved by the solitary setting of her magnificent mountain residence.

Nose for it, the old sixth sense? It crossed Schiapin's mind that the lady might not be unconnected with the Italians' mysterious presence in Goeschenen. He needed proof, and he obtained it the very same afternoon.

From his look-out post at his bedroom window, at about four o'clock, he sighted an imposing carriage halting before the entrance to the Adler. The coachman enquired, quite audibly, whether 'Signor Vigliotti' was within. A moment later down the steps came Signor Vigliotti (and he was Clara's fiancé). Collecting an envelope which the coachman held out, he took one look at it and said: 'I'll deliver it.'

As fast as his legs could carry him Schiapin scampered downstairs and was just in time to see the carriage vanish round a corner of the hotel. He went in pursuit. The carriage was pulling up outside the *Bierstube*: the coachman was thirsty. Schiapin meantime ran an appreciative eye, and hand, over the unusually handsome pair of horses, and when the coachman reappeared paid him a compliment.

'Hungarian, aren't they? And so beautifully cared for. My congratulations.'

The coachman was not unmoved. And Schiapin, by now sure of his man, announced in his best German:

'Frau Von Goltz certainly knows how to choose. Her horses and her servants.'

'That's a fact, sir. There's not a woman to touch her in all Uri Canton.'

So his journalist's curiosity was rewarded with two vital titbits in one day: that a short way from Goeschenen resided a beautiful lady, a millionairess of cosmopolitan habits, and that the beautiful lady had urgent, confidential messages to send to one of the four Italians. Signor X, probably.

There remained a lesser enigma: the Bernardo Gherardini to

which Count Della Gherardesca had allowed himself to be humbled in order to oblige (in what way? for what reason?) the so-called Moriana. That apart, the solution to the mystery was rather trite. Downright disappointing. The usual 'cherchez la femme'.

Next morning he was awoken by a knock on his door at eight o'clock. The telegram from Rome. Brief but sufficient. 'Gherardesca still president of APER but due to resign owing to pressure of new duties i.e. since December attached to Sovereign's civil establishment. Currently not in Rome or Monza. Good luck.'

The first idea to occur to him had no sensational implications. Della Gherardesca was now above all suspicion, having been elevated to the limbo of the royal circle, which could justify all manner of things. He was on holiday with two other court functionaries together with some high-up dignitary, 'Signor X'. The Minister for the Royal Household, let us suppose, or some such figure.

It looked like it was going to be a splendid day. He dressed, then opened the window. And there, on the terrace ten feet below him, he saw Signor X himself, a coffee cup in his hand. He was on his feet, standing with his back to the view. Satisfied, benign. Looking very relaxed in a white twill suit. Not far from him an elderly foreign lady was commencing her matutinal devotions to the Alps, manoeuvring the hotel telescope in an attempt to focus on the dazzling mysteries of the Dammafirn glacier. Signor X stepped over to her and offered his binoculars.

'Try these,' he said in French. 'Zeiss, a first-rate instrument.'

On an impulse which was quite mechanical Schiapin felt for his wallet, took a 20 lira note from it, and compared the two.

The 'discovery', his success in recognising the man, was not so much a visual achievement as the result of a mental observation. Between the portrait on the banknote and the original before his eyes there was no connection at all: the personage in the portrait was august and brooding while the reality was simply a well-dressed and well-preserved representative of the bourgeoisie. Pleased to be enjoying the morning at a 'beauty spot' far from the madding crowd.

But quite aside from his portrait, the man did not even resemble his own person at that particular moment. He was an unconvincing double of himself. Too radiant and bronzed, rejuvenated, recharged. Even his closest acquaintances would have had trouble recognising him instantly. As for Schiapin, transfixed in the window with that 20 lira note in his hand, the thought which was uppermost in his mind was slightly disconcerting: Our image of him is rather better.

Signor X left the terrace. Doubtless he had weighty matters to attend to, what with responding to Frau Von Goltz's urgent messages, and Clara's pleading looks. Schiapin saw him next, brushed against him in fact, as he was entering the dining-room on the second bell. He felt no thrill at all.

He did not think of himself as a supporter of the Republicans, far from it. The monarchy was mere form, in his opinion, and so insubstantial that anything whose *raison d'être* was to oppose it could not but be equally irrelevant and immaterial. He was of the opinion (his half-English blood inclined him towards empiricism) that the lottery-booths and the law courts, the universities and salt-and-tobacco dispensers, the penitentiaries and the barracks, the Quirinal cuirassiers and the taxmen of Vicenza, the *camorristi* of Avellino and the councillors in the State Audit Court, following the substitution of a Phrygian cap for a crown on the Head of State, would all remain precisely as before. And so, of course, would the subjects turned citizens. But even though he was lukewarm towards the idea of a Republic he also felt lukewarm, at least to the same degree, towards the King. The gentleman whom from his table he observed doing battle with a portion of *Trockenfleisch* did not arouse in him feelings of either fervour or fury. An irrelevant figure, as incapable of doing harm as he was of doing good, as neutral and colourless as the seal embossed on state notepaper.

But Schiapin was a journalist, and from that angle the matter was not without its value. This fortuitous encounter was a major scoop. It was big news.

Leaving his ex-flame to her own devices (visible on the other side of a glass partition discreetly dividing her attentions between her future husband and His Sovereign Majesty the King of Italy) he got on with writing up his 'story', right there in the reading-room where they had served him his *café-crème*. The lead-in paragraph cost him little effort. 'Confidential, not to say privileged, information divulged exclusively to this newspaper has enabled us to trace to his otherwise untraceable *buen retiro* in Switzerland a Very Important Person. We have dared to unmask an incognito, our evidence is watertight . . .' The rest of it would not fill more than thirty lines of print and it described the locality without revealing it, referred to Frau Von Goltz in all but name, and alluded to the 'promising friendship' linking her to the 'august tourist'. It omitted to mention the presence (and enterprise) of Clara Mansolin.

A few technical points for the editor: two-column headline, adequate type, to be brought out on page 2, not too prominent, possibly add: 'We intend to supply, all being well, further news more fully documenting our *intimate revelations*.' Sign: 'WS'.

By the time 'WS' left the reading-room to make his way to the telegraph office Signorina Mansolin had dispatched (no doubt in her inimitable fashion) her future husband. She was rapt in contemplation of Signor X's furrowed brow, as he immersed himself in the most demanding of his labours, Three Club solitaire.

With a slightly bitter taste in his mouth Schiapin walked through the village, in the dazzle of the glaciers which today seemed to explode out of the black roofs. His story had to go by ordinary telegraph, the Goeschenen office never having heard of such things as press telegrams. He was wrong, however, to let his ill-humour get the better of him. On his way back he noticed, standing at the corner of the road from the station, a pretty lass in travel-clothes, with a generous figure and copper-coloured hair, a suitcase in one hand and a coat over her arm. Setting down the case she shaded her eyes with her fan. Margaretha? Never! But it was, it was. Margaretha the impatient. Margaretha the generous. Margaretha the vengeful.

Schiapin had long since ceased to be surprised at feminine perspicacity. His system was to forestall it.

'Well, *Liebling*. She's blonde and twenty-one.'

'Oh! I imagined she was a brunette.'

'Whichever, you're going to tear my eyes out, aren't you?'

'Or something else. Is there a room for me in your hotel? I intend to see this blonde, I do.'

'And first I intend to show you I haven't wasted myself on any blondes. And by the by, here's the proof I've been here strictly in a professional capacity. The receipt for a telegram. I've just telegraphed an item to the paper.'

'Did you have to be three days about it?'

'I did indeed. I've caught a monster sea-serpent. A real live one too.'

He had translated the Italian expression literally into German, and she failed to understand.

'What do you mean? A serpent?'

'I mean I had sensational news to send in. Concerning a Very Important Person.'

'The tenor Tamagno?'

'No, and not even Thomas Edison. Higher up, much higher up. A serpent with a crown on his head. I'll tell you all about it when we get there.'

But when she saw the hotel she changed her mind. She pointed at Herr Wüntz.

'Who's he?'

'The proprietor.'

'No, this is no place for us. Don't you see the way he's staring at us? Worse than my boss in the bank. Do you mind if we leave right away? We'll be in Küsnacht by tonight.'

'I was intending to give you that proof right now.'

'I'll accept the first instalment on the train, if we're alone. I like it.'

The separate compartments on the trains of that era, disagreeable to sufferers from claustrophobia, offered certain advantages to lovers.

VIII

───────────── • ─────────────

The print on the wall beside his bed often caught his eye, and after his siesta, towel round his neck, the Count stopped to examine it. Aged five, aged ten, fifteen, twenty, twenty-five, thirty: all on the upward trend, and at thirty-five you are midway, at the peak. The decline sets in at forty, by forty-five you are well on your way, and thereafter it's a straight tumble, all the way to the bottom. Thus the *Stufenalter des Mannes*, the pyramid or parable of the Ages of a Man, the oleograph found in every corner of the Teutonic world, from the Gotthard to the Baltic.

Each step or age has its caption, and caustic enough where appropriate, with all due allowance for the popular, homespun idiom. The final ones are catastrophic, utterly devastating. For the forty-five year old, stumbling, obese, bespectacled, greying, a bottle of wine under one arm: 'Feeling his vital juices go – He has no more wild oats to sow. – Spurned by wife and woman next-door – He makes his bed on the tavern floor.'

Signor Moriana would not have been capable of a translation even as rough and ready as ours, but the crude naivety of the illustration rendered it superfluous. He glared at the print with a no less naive hatred, and then turned round to Mancuso.

'Here, take down that picture and get rid of it.'

'Where?'

'Anywhere you like. Take it to the proprietor, sling it in the river.'

Mancuso lifted the picture off its nail.

'Signor Conte, I was instructed by Count Della Gherar . . .'

'Ssh!'

'By Signor Gherardini . . . He says he wishes to be received by you.'

'Tell him to go the Kiosk and wait for me there.'

The three of them – Gherardesca, Brighenti and he – each had a favourite haunt for a cup of coffee or a drink. Gherardesca liked the Hotel Des Alpes, a small establishment at the other end of the village, Brighenti who knew German was fond of the hotel *Bierstube* where he could hobnob with the locals, while the Count's favourite retreat was the kiosk midway along the Larchwood Promenade, beside the river.

A bit of a hitch had arisen over the Visé sale, that was the substance of what Gherardesca had to tell him, having finally decided to break the news after two days of hesitation and a consultation with Brighenti. Administration, belatedly notified of the sale, had reported that a mortgage had been taken out on the castle and grounds. For 150,000. And it had been running for five or six years already.

The Count did not seem unduly alarmed.

'Well, who took it out?'

'You must have raised it yourself, Count. Only the owner has the right.'

'Me? I had better things to raise. No, I have an infallible memory, you know. And I have no recollection of anything of the sort. Anyhow, what's this mortgage going to mean?'

Obviously it ought to be redeemed at once, or else the purchaser would have to be informed. So that she could take it over, naturally after negotiating a corresponding adjustment to the price of the sale.

'So, what's our best move?'

'I would suggest we charge Vigliotti to broach the matter with the lady. To enter into discussions with her as soon as possible and absolutely frankly.'

'Get someone to go and find him.'

One of Vigliotti's virtues was that he was always easily found. Ten minutes later there he was, silent, solemn, immaculate. The Count gave orders and instructions, emphasising that he should leave as soon as he could. As he addressed him he did not take his eyes off him, but the Count could read nothing in his face. Did he object to having to go, being told to quit Clara's side? Nothing. Inscrutable. What a fellow, he said to himself, I don't see him commanding a cruiser but he has everything required of a good diplomat, I'll make him an ambassador some day.

Vigliotti had not stirred.

'Any further orders?'

'Yes, assure Frau Von Goltz that I am very grateful for the invitation. For the stag. Before I leave he'll get what's coming to him.'

'And the Frau too,' he added, *sotto voce*.

By five o'clock Vigliotti was already on his way to Wassen.

Later that evening. Reading-room of the Hotel Adler, after dinner. (Not one of the residents has noticed the departure of that slim, restless Englishman, Mr Fairtales.)

The Count is relaxing in an armchair, a newspaper spread before him. Enter Clara. She performs the semblance of a curtsy, then whispers:

'Big surprise. The Indian Mail is coming through.'

'Where?'

'At 8.15 at the station. Aren't you going to come, Signor Conte?'

Orphaned, so he had learned, and shut up in a convent run by Grey Sisters for six years. This evening, with her fair hair swept back in two wings and held in a bun, lorgnette dangling on a gold chain, she resembled nothing so much as a schoolmistress.

'It only comes through twice a month!'

In the V of her neckline, as he was rising from his chair, his gaze lit on the rosy swell of her bosom.

'Put those papers away. What use are they to you, Count?'

What indeed.

Not until they were at the station did it occur to him to notice that Frau Schwartz was absent.

'*Je l'ai renvoyée, elle est de tout temps enrhumée.* And now she's in love as well! Oh, Count, you'll never guess who with. Head over heels! *La pauvre.*'

'That's enough of that.'

He was impervious to gossip, even when the topic was Princess Bonaparte. In Rome and in Monza it was common knowledge, and commented upon with endless amazement by informers and gossip-mongers.

The unwanted third party was absent, furthermore Clara had wrapped a plaid around her shoulders. Not a shawl, a great thick plaid which the cool of the evening could scarcely be said to warrant. The kind of thing which when spread out softly in a meadow is as good as a double bed. It was to provide the Count with much food for thought a little later on.

In good time the Indian Mail appeared, preluded by a deafening din, the whole valley reverberating to the sound of the locomotives puffing up the long gradient. The famous armoured train, fleeting and mysterious, consisted of two sleeping-cars and two baggage vans with sentries riding on the end platforms and it linked London to Brindisi via Ostend, Basle and Bologna, carrying officials, mail and valuables destined for the East. At Brindisi an extra-fast steamer would be waiting, ready to sail full steam ahead for the Suez Canal.

'Just think! All the way from London to Calcutta only takes them twelve days. My goodness, what miracles we are living to see!'

The Count noticed that the engines being topped up with water were larger than the customary ones. Even Swiss Railways were impressed by the might of Great Britain and those initials 'VR' gleaming in gold against the blue of the carriages. One or two passengers appeared, behind the brightly-lit windows. Although they were out of uniform his practised eye recognised them with no difficulty: army officers. But the halt was very short. The train set off again in the direction of the tunnel, which was ready to swallow it in a moment.

Ah, now they were free, my word. In which direction should he take her? He would have to think up something. Along the Larchwood Promenade, past the kiosk (half a kilometre, no more) was a little clearing in the hillside, he could remember the exact spot. It could be just right for the purpose, no one would be around.

And she, meek as a lamb, let him lead the way. They crossed the bridge over the Reuss, in the thick deep dust of the carriage road. Darkness, silence. One way or another they would have to pass in front of the Adler, and negotiate the powerful acetylene lighting.

'Not a word, I beg you. Keep to this side of the road, right behind me.'

'Follow my finger and you can't miss it. No muck in the air, up here in the Alps. See it: Andromeda, then the Swan. Go a bit further over and that's the Lyre, with Vega.'

And who else could it be but his illustrious Personal Secretary, confound him? Giving astronomy lessons in the hotel drive. For the edification of the schoolmistress from Zürich.

He stopped, stretching out an arm to warn Clara. Too late. Already they were within the bright circle of lights. And Clara's white blouse stood out a mile.

And meanwhile that dunderhead, who put on the thickest Tuscan accent as soon as he was out of earshot of his Boss:

'Arcturus, now there's a little fellow it isn't so easy to spot.'

The Count in his dark suit escaped his eye, but Clara he sighted at once.

'Come on over here and join us, Signorina. What are you hiding over there for?'

'Imbecile!' hissed the Boss.

There was nothing for it. He had to cross the road and be recognised. But it was she who saved the situation, in the most matter-of-fact manner.

'We were up at the station. The Indian Mail has just been through. The Count met an Englishman he knows. Lord . . .'

'Balfour,' he swore. But consoled himself with the thought that her incriminating lie was an admission. A promise.

Meantime, goodnight. Clara went straight upstairs, leaving him to his bitter thoughts. And sweet: that plaid she had specially prepared, and how adorable she had been this evening, his little schoolmistress, all anticipation, and now alone in her room with this passion that he had aroused, her secret desires. Thoughts to keep a man awake all night, set every fibre of his being on fire.

Instead he slept like a log, the curse or the blessing of those forty-five years, right through from eleven until six in the morning. At seven he was already out and about, walking. Never mind the *Stufenalter des Mannes*, he was bursting with health, up there in that little valley below the Dammastock.

Well, what about business? The mortgage? Might it not help things along if he put a word in too? A client such as La Goltz deserved it, some proof of his esteem. After all, it would only mean sacrificing half a day on her account. By the early hours of the afternoon he would be back in Goeschenen, providing there were no unforeseen developments. The only one he ruled out being the stag; today he was in no mood for blowing holes in old stags.

He had a word with the hotel porter, who booked him a carriage.

By 9.30 they were in Wassen, or rather the coachman set him down a little before the village, higher up, and he continued his way on foot by a path leading off the highroad (beside a wayside inn) straight down to Villa Goltz; the very same route Mr Fairtales had followed two days previously. He instructed the coachman to wait for him at the same point, adding that if he didn't show up by three he was free to go back without him.

It was another glorious day, and as he walked down the path he could see a little church ahead. In that remote era of the railway it was a familiar landmark to travellers from all over Europe. For then travel by train was a thrill which the railway companies fostered by devising ingenious circuitous routes, spectacular ascents and descents and contortions, fruit of a technology full of fantasy which, like the opera-house, prized set design and *trompe-l'oeil* effects purely for their own sakes. After the great long tunnel the Gotthard line exhibited an extraordinary series of virtuoso convolutions as it sank gradually into the great bowel of Wassen, green with pine-forests and bristling with glaciers high above. The train would emerge from the mountain and traverse the entire valley by viaduct to pierce the mountain on the other side, coming out into the daylight again hundreds of feet lower down to recross the valley in the reverse direction, so that passengers saw the little church of Wassen successively on their right and on their left, at first far beneath their feet and then high up, lost among the rocks above their heads. Needless to say, nothing was further from Signor Moriana's mind than that panorama.

He was pondering the mortgage. Possibly his emissary had not been too well received. The whole Visé deal might be in jeopardy. The one Italian word which all foreigners know is *imbroglio*: La Goltz might very well have had recourse to it already, and not without justification either, seeing there was no reason for her to be well-acquainted with our legal terminology and attendant cavils.

In effect she had been sold goods which were not entirely the seller's to dispose of. Apart from the very poor figure he risked cutting, there was reason to fear that she might rescind the contract. True, there was hope too. Vigliotti might manage to sugar the pill and persuade her to swallow it. This should not be beyond a negotiator of his calibre.

And to all appearance his hope was not unfounded.

Because at a certain point where the track cut straight across a great sloping meadow – fresh-mown, beautiful, lying there between the pines – at the edge of the field, down at the bottom end, the Count caught sight of something which made him halt abruptly and slip behind a tree-trunk. And his binoculars confirmed that there was nothing the matter with his vision. In that hammock slung between two pines was the lady herself, Frau Von Goltz.

She was leaning out of the hammock and her bare arms were drawing towards her, tenderly, the figure of a man standing close beside her. And she kissed him, she kissed him again and again. An enchanting spectacle, in its morning Alpine setting. Also a not unencouraging spectacle, for him, at that particular juncture in his meditations. Because the object of La Goltz's effusions was none other than Vigliotti. His negotiator.

He kept his binoculars trained on the little scene (which did not alter) a moment or two longer and then withdrew, backing away trunk by trunk, before turning to climb the path again. He had

had no option but to abandon the field; the role of old stag had fallen to him.

Not until he reached the *Gasthaus* did he finally sit down and have a rest. To pass the time he decided to remain there for lunch, in the interim submitting to the courteous approaches of a Swiss (French-Swiss) gentleman who had noted his arrival and evidently needed someone to chat to.

Overflowing with a sonorous and extravagant Italian the man enthused without interruption upon the inexhaustible marvels of the Alpine scenery, the golden future for hotels, the only local industry, the perfection of the season (never mind that it had rained nearly every day), the Gotthard highroad, a veritable European artery (no matter that in the past hour nothing but the Wassen mail-coach had passed). He touched upon some items of society gossip, and also literature. Then he got onto politics.

'You see, the trouble with our Confederation is that it has no politics to speak of. No foreign policy.'

He went on to recount how a few days earlier in Lausanne, his native city, he had attended one of the sessions of the Congress of European Republicans.

'You Italians were very under-represented. I saw only three or four of your people, including Cavallotti. No more than that. What I believe you would call in Italian *quattro gatti*, just four cats. Why so? Don't they want a Republic in your country?'

The Count poured himself, and also the other man, a second glass of Martini.

'Four cats, you say. That's plenty enough, because the mouse has gone soft in the head. It's on its last legs.'

'The Monarchy, you mean?'

'What else?'

They ate at the same table, the loquacious Swiss proving himself of a most generous disposition by absolutely insisting on paying for his newfound foreign friend's meal.

'One day I'll come to Italy and you can return the compliment in your own home.'

'You can bank on that.'

Back at the Adler no one was waiting for him. None of his entourage, that is. Instead waiting for him at the porter's desk was a voluminous envelope inscribed: *Signor Contè Di Moriana – Goeschenen, Canton Uri, CH.*

'It was left for you by a gentleman who arrived by train.'

'From where?'

'I couldn't say. He spoke with a German accent, had lunch here and then left again on the two o'clock. The northbound express.'

'Is Signor Gherardini out?'

He was.

'As soon as he gets back send him up to my room.'

He did not get back for an hour, and boldly braved the Chief's inevitable ire.

'We assumed, Count, that you would be lunching away. We organised a little picnic. In the woods.'

'With the ladies?'

'With Frau Tschudi and Frau Schwartz. Signorina Mansolin decided to stay in the hotel.'

Signor Conte Di Moriana's face brightened.

'When we're back in Monza you will get your holiday. Here, my dear Gherardini, you must resign yourself to the fact that you are on duty. Open this envelope, would you.'

The envelope contained a second one, with the same inscription but written in a different hand and bearing arms and seals which Gherardesca recognised instantly. He opened it and drew forth a sheet of paper.

'It's from Kaiser Wilhelm.'

It concluded with the signature 'Wilhelm IR' and began with the words *'Lieber Vetter'* (Dear Cousin), and was dated 'Friedrichshafen, 8 September'. The text itself was a good side and a half long. The writing was very clear and regular, and yet that page and a half of German prose was an ocean upon which neither he nor Gherardesca would have dreamed of venturing.

With Vigliotti absent the only one of them up to the task was Brighenti, the Herr Professor. Summoned at once to the Count's room, Brighenti read the missive aloud with all due solemnity, and slowness, and then translated. Or paraphrased.

'The Emperor is on Lake Constance, at Friedrichshafen, and he says that he is taking some time off from his duties. He says that

Friedrichshafen is only a few hours' journey from the place where the Count is presently residing. Then, he will never forget the gratifying and welcoming, or shall we say gratifying and cordial, days of his visit to Rome a year ago. "A truly unforgettable royal and popular welcome." Which deepens, which strengthens, the warm relations existing. Persisting between the two nations. Between the two monarchies and the two peoples. And he says "I should like", or more exactly "I should appreciate to the highest degree", "to the most appropriate degree I should appreciate". Or rather: "I should consider most appreciable".'

'Go on!'

Brighenti wiped his spectacles and his brow. And went on:

'"I should considerably appreciate the opportunity of an unprepared meeting." Unprepared, unscheduled.'

'Come on, what's written there? That he wants to see me? Is he coming here?'

For some time the Count had been pacing to and fro in the room in evident agitation. He suddenly halted in front of poor Brighenti and gave him a thunderous look. Gherardesca thought to himself: It's his desperate desire to be honoured by a visit from his powerful ally.

'Yes or no? Get to the point!'

'I very much regret to have to say this, Count, but the answer is no. The Emperor is not coming. I presume he does not have the opportunity, the time. It ends like this: "With affectionate respect". No, "humble respect". And then all good wishes for your sojourn in Switzerland. If you wish I'll translate the last part word for word for you. "I am pleased to renew my feelings of". Or better, "the expression of my feelings of . . ."'

'We know all that!' the Count cut in, and sat down on a chair.

A pause, pregnant with implications, while, as every day at that hour, a smell of boiling fat drifted through the open windows.

'Can you absolutely assure me His Majesty is not coming?'

'Absolutely. In the letter . . .'

'Good. I leave you the letter, trusting in your most scrupulous discretion. You will return it to me together with a written translation.'

'By when, Count?'

'You can have twenty-four hours.'

When the two men left he began to appraise the enormity of the danger he had escaped.

His second meeting with the young Wilhelm had been as recent as May, in Berlin this time, and it had given him every ground for developing to invincible proportions the aversion which he had first felt for the man in Rome in '88. It was an antipathy which was in no way reciprocated. Wilhelm kept on writing to him, paying him compliments, citing his name in official speeches, proposing more talks. He had no inkling that the more he persisted the worse it was, not having the remotest suspicion that his 'Cousin' could possibly hold against him, before all else, the indefatigable enthusiasm and missionary zeal with which he performed his role of Sovereign. A job which his Cousin, for his part, carried out with congenital distaste, the most profound resentment and weariness.

No *raisons d'état* explained this dislike (he did not have such a high opinion of himself as to question the wisdom of the political luminaries, the eternal fathers as he called them, who had chosen to ally Italy with Germany). Nor did the disparity in their ages – Wilhelm was not yet thirty – have anything to do with it, nor even the generic difference in temperament between a Prussian and a Piedmontese by now thoroughly Italianised. His dislike was instinctive, deeply felt, and totally free of self-interest.

That Wilhelm had renounced the idea of visiting him in Goeschenen had to be accounted little short of a miracle. Only one other person he knew could match the Kaiser's mania for travel and that was his own Duchess, La Litta. Per month the imperial train burnt the same amount of coal as the *Deutschland*, the biggest steamer in the Hamburg-Amerika Line, or so a Munich newspaper had claimed, and the exaggeration was not totally implausible. From this point of view Wilhelm displayed a distinctly modern temperament, even somewhat feminine: this nervous restlessness, movement for the pure and simple desire, never satisfied, to be on the move.

To come charging up into these mountains to turn the whole place upside down for one day, for two days, affronting Swiss neutrality with his performing *troupe* of bodyguards in silver breastplates and gilt helmets, his generals and his ministers, preceded by an advance party of swallow-tailed flunkeys and aides, secretaries and sundry other hangers-on – the notion would have crossed his mind, without a doubt. And he had to thank all the saints in heaven that some graver task, some bolder project, had driven it out of his head.

Alone in his room, the Count took off his jacket and slackened his belt, still scowling.

Standing before the open window he did his fifteen minutes of physical jerks, his bending and stretching exercises. In Goeschenen there was no opportunity for riding, and yet here in Goeschenen he had particular reasons for needing to keep specially fit, slim, trim, quick off the mark.

He bathed and shaved. Shave twice a day, a little secret that makes all the difference. Mancuso had laid out a dark suit for him, and a dark tie. No, no, none of that: summer colours, fresh and inviting colours. And then outdoors, into the free air, amid the larches – to breathe again, to live.

And to meet his Clara.

No Clara.

She was not to be found in the village, although he spotted Frau Schwartz in her black veil going into church. Nor was she in the hotel, at least not in any of its public rooms. It was past five o'clock, perhaps she was in her room. He remembered how it had been she who had told him which one it was. An invitation, clearly. Should he go? Not for the first time would he be knocking on a woman's door. But here they were in a hotel. What if La Schwartz should come back, or if there were any hotel staff in the vicinity? Or if the little thing had changed her mind . . . Little thing? She was a woman. Twenty-one years old. And had he not kissed her already? Up there in the tunnel. And had his kiss not met with prompt (and swollen, and penetrating) collaboration from her mouth?

The urge was strong, poor man. The vestige of sangfroid restraining him, the last-minute prompting of prudence, inspired him to grab his binoculars. And then up he went. At the start of the corridor down which lay number 13 he paused a moment to get back his breath after all the stairs, and just as well for him. Clara, in a flannel bath-wrap, issued from her bedroom door at that same moment and went through the door opposite her own. She was too short-sighted to have noticed him.

It was the door to the bathroom. He heard the bath being filled and then his ears detected a tiny noise, watery too but from a different source, and the thought of it made the blood rush to his head. He heard her get in, the full length of her body surrendering to the heat. Splashing sounds . . . It was a quick bath. Minutes later Clara was crossing the corridor again, in a soap-scented cloud, rubber bathcap dripping. Now that she was not laced in a corset she exhibited the beginnings of a little paunch. So that was why at table she declined the *pommes frites* and whipped cream, and the *knöpfli*, the potato dumplings. Very tasty all the same, no two ways about it.

Her surprise was completely genuine.

'Oh!' And it took her a moment to recover. 'So you are back.'

'I was only in Wassen.'

'For you, Signor Conte, Wassen seems to hold a lot of attractions.'

Desire generally made him more perceptive. He noted that she had not said 'for you as well'. So she was not thinking about Vigliotti, not yet.

'I assure you there is only one place in Switzerland that has any attraction for me. This corridor.'

'Oh no. That's not possible.'

'*Vous me connaissez*, Clara . . .'

He reached out a hand to close a gap in her bath-robe across her bosom. She blushed chastely, aware that certain gestures in a man mean the very opposite to what they seem.

Nonetheless she meant to ascertain that Signor Di Moriana had not completely lost his head, a thing which is disagreeable (to women), even off-putting.

'So what really brought you up here?'

'You have my full permission not to believe it, but I came to get a better view of the glacier. The Dammafirn.'

'Those two American climbers?'

'Those two American climbers.'

Appreciating his quick thinking, Clara understood she would have to concede him something, and rubbed herself against him. Unmistakably. On the pretext of wanting to look out of the window.

'Will you lend me your binoculars?'

'Have them. They're yours.'

And he left her. He had come very close to losing his head. But so far it was still on his shoulders.

Two hours later, as he was crossing the lobby (where there were other people) on his way to dinner he heard from the next-door room the first bars of the Royal March. It put him right off his stride, at first. Right off. But when he looked into the room he broke into a smile. He ran to the piano and reached out, rather incongruously, to put a hand over her mouth. Her lips pressed kisses on those harsh fingers which sought to seal them. And after dinner came the second miracle, following that of being spared the imperial visitation. He actually listened to music. The girl, admittedly, was inspired in her choice and had the good sense not to drag it out too long. A few excerpts of Liszt and then straight into Emmanuel Chabrier. The Count really seemed to be quite taken with it. When she nodded her head he turned the score for her, his hand brushing her cheek. And each page turned was rewarded by a fleeting kiss on the back of his hand.

'This,' he reflected to himself, 'is what in the language of today is called "flirtation". All right for tiny tots. Tomorrow we'll get on to more serious business.'

Early next morning, just as he was about to set off hunting, they showed him a letter from Frau Von Goltz, addressed to Gherardesca. The lady wrote to say that she and her administrator, Herr Grüber, were considering 'the little unforeseen complication', and she asked to be excused 'for being compelled to detain Signor Vigliotti'.

Gherardesca ventured to express his cautious confidence that things would sort themselves out all right in the end.

'There's no doubt they will,' the Count reassured him. 'You'll see. All's going to go swimmingly.'

Gherardesca reported this to Brighenti, concluding: 'Mountain air must suit the liverish. Our man has become an optimist.'

'Fiddlesticks. Mountain air is no good for hepatic complaints. It's the peumus leaf infusion I get him to take every evening. And the cholagogues, and the cascara laxatives.'

But their man truly was in good spirits. Even high spirits. Stirred by fond memories of schoolboy reading ('Rinaldo imprisoned in Armida's castle'). In the mood for a boyish prank.

He asked them to let him have a sheet of paper in the Bureau. '*Ma petite*,' he wrote. '*On te couronne avant de te faire reine.*' No more. After adding Signorina Mansolin's name and surname to the envelope he popped it in the pigeon-hole for number 13, and went out to join the other hunters in the drive.

He regretted it immediately. Back in he went and pulled out the note and tore it up. A joke is all very well, but *billets doux* of that sort, and unsigned? Sheer madness. For a start, she wouldn't have believed it. And even if she had imagined something of the kind was in his mind, if she suspected it, nothing would be achieved by writing to her. He looked up and saw Frau Schwartz standing in the lobby. He called out her name.

'Tell the Signorina that Vigliotti has to stay in Wassen. I have no idea when he will be free.'

Thus far he could go: perfectly correct behaviour, irreproachable. Merely notifying the anxious maiden that her betrothed was detained in Wassen for close (close!) discussions with La Goltz. Meantime he would see to it that Rinaldo got his just desserts, on the poor betrayed damsel's account and on his own (Vigliotti had trespassed on his preserve, even if admittedly he was only a reluctant poacher). Accounts, in short, were being settled, in the expectation of settling the Visé business (for which he was forced to rely on Rinaldo himself and his unexpected collusion with the other party: a first-class *imbroglio*, in Swiss territory but typically Italian).

His head labouring with these complicated thoughts, he set off for the hunt, which this time did not look like being particularly long or arduous. The previous evening, hardly a stone's throw from the hotel, people had noticed themselves being eyed by two chamois, male and female, only just above the carriage road. The reason was the fine weather which had allowed the farmers to make hay on the higher meadows, reducing the grazing there for the animals.

At 12.30, still in corduroy but punctual, the Count and Gherardesca were seated in the dining-room for luncheon, although they had left no earlier than 8 o'clock. On the doorstep of his hotel a satisfied Herr Wüntz stood watch over the victims displayed beside the entrance. The huge eyes of the two chamois, male and female, had not yet misted over. They were still asking, vainly, why.

'Why?' he said, lowering his voice. 'The answer is very simple. To come up and see the view. Just as I did yesterday.'

'But do you want me to wait for you in the corridor?'

'Wait for me behind the door of your room. You can recognise my step, can't you?'

'I'd recognise your breath.'

'When I'm a bit out of puff, eh? Well, what time will Frau Schwartz be going out?'

'About four.'

'I'll be there before five.'

'And you're going to stay out in the corridor?'

'I'll come in, if you prefer. I'll come in, I'll come in! Were you not saying you couldn't find that music by Offenbach? We can look for it together. Nice light music, you know, more my style.'

And as he undressed in his room preparatory to taking a bit of a nap he mentally reviewed the ritual objections, and the time-honoured replies. 'But sir, you propose to rob me of the most precious thing I have.' Reply: 'You will be rewarded.' 'But sir, you will get me into trouble.' 'Never fear, I'll defend you.' There was a third possible line of resistance, and here the appropriate peremptory reply was suggested to him by a distant Savoy forebear, Prince Eugene. 'But sir, I am the wife of one of your officers.' 'Madam, I do not detract from my officers' honour by bedding their wives. I enhance it.'

Anyhow, had not his own father once said to Count Benso Di Cavour: 'Origins of the nobility? Half trash, half cash. And the whole lot mishmash.'

He fell sound asleep.

One person who was far from asleep at that hour, one floor above the Count's, was Brighenti. Having double-locked his door he had taken the Imperial epistle from the drawer in his bedside table and settled down to compile his written translation. First of all he took the trouble to make a fair copy of the German text, to keep it as a historical curio. His translation went along well for the first two-thirds of the letter. Then he hit a snag.

Gracious, what a nasty business. That sentence. How had he translated it for the Count, that one little phrase? Goodness gracious me (and his forehead was suddenly beaded with sweat). He had given a wrong translation. Wrong, completely wrong. He read it over again. And again. No two ways about it, he had been totally and utterly mistaken.

He replaced the sheet of paper, groped in the half-light for his hat and stick in the corner and dashed out. Luckily, as he learned from the porter, Gherardesca had left the hotel only a minute or two earlier. But there was no sign of him anywhere. Where the devil had he got to?

Little did he know that it was no use looking for him anywhere in the village. With Mancuso for guide Gherardesca was also searching high and low, for his cartridge belt which he had mislaid that morning somewhere up in the woods behind the station at the end of the hunt. When they finally bumped into each other it was gone half past four.

'Quick! He's coming!' Brighenti burst out, grabbing him by the arm.

'What?'

'He's coming. I got it wrong!'

'But who?'

'Wilhelm! The Kaiser!'

'But yesterday he said he wasn't coming.'

'A v'deggh ch'al vèin!' said Brighenti breaking into the dialect in his agitation. 'I tell you he's coming. Get back to the hotel and warn him.'

'The Count? You go yourself, you're the one who botched it up.'

'Not me, my friend. Who is his Secretary? I'm the physician.'

Well, all it really came down to was a matter of delivering some good news, and Gherardesca was of a noble disposition as well as blood.

'So when's he due to arrive, the Emperor?'

'He isn't clear about that. Who knows, it could be tomorrow.'

The Chief had just stepped out of the bath-tub and was starting to pull his clothes back on, with Mancuso standing by to give him a shave (always shave twice a day, one of those little details that makes all the difference), when Gherardesca knocked on his door.

He had been prepared for a bit of a rebuke, at the very worst. Instead Gherardesca was confronted with the spectacle of a man in the throes of nervous collapse.

IX

────────── • ──────────

In a shirt with no collar, and his underpants, the Count dropped
back onto the chair. Groaning. He did not even have the strength
to dismiss his man. It was Gherardesca who motioned to Mancuso to make himself scarce.

'My poor holiday! This little breather I was allowing myself
just so that I could keep going.'

'But the Emperor is doing you an honour. Very flattering
too.'

'Ah, why am I so unlucky?'

'He is showing you proof of his friendship, Count.'

Like talking to a brick wall. The man could do nothing but
moan and despair.

'He'll feed me to the lions. To the newspapers. All of Europe
will know. He's ruined everything, can't you see?'

'We'll do what we can to keep the press out of it.'

'And that's not all. Wilhelm will want to see La Goltz, and then
La Goltz will blab the whole story of the mortgage. For me it's a
disaster, I tell you. Believe me.'

Exasperated by him up to this point, Gherardesca began to pity
him. Sincerely.

'Don't worry about the mortgage. We'll tell Vigliotti not to
leave the lady's side for a moment, if Wilhelm decides to pay a call
to Wassen. The Emperor has a bee in his bonnet about the
navy . . .'

'A bee?'

'Precisely, sir. And Vigliotti is a naval officer, is he not? If Frau

Von Goltz brings up the subject of Visé, Vigliotti starts in on the navy. "We are presently testing a new type of torpedo, the most powerful in the world." Wilhelm's ears prick up, the conversation takes a different turn. So you mustn't give yourself any worries on that score, Signor Conte. Vigliotti is a very smart chap.'

The first ray of hope. He starts pulling on his trousers.

'You think he can avoid . . .'

'Beyond a shadow of doubt.'

'That Vigliotti! Is he always fated to be my saviour?'

'You can easily show your appreciation.'

'That I can. If he gets me out of this pickle he'll be returning to Italy with the rank of Commander. But we have to let him know what's happening.'

'I'll go. I'll leave at once. Carriage or train, I'll be in Wassen by six.'

'And you'll report straight back tonight. Gherardesca, you are a true friend.'

'Much obliged, Signor Conte.'

'That Vigliotti', to whom he had to remember to show his appreciation. But first of all, by an odd quirk of fate, he had to pay a call on the man's fiancée, in her bedroom. And with one thing and another it had slipped his mind. What was the time? The pitiless hands of his Vacheron-Constantin pointed to 5.25. For fully twenty-five minutes Clara had been standing waiting for him behind her door, perhaps trembling. There was no time for him to finish dressing.

Pulling on his dressing-gown he set out, along the maze of stairs and corridors and more stairs that separated his own room from number 13. He was almost there when just ahead of him he saw a figure ascending the stairs. Frau Schwartz. The chaperon. What now?

'Signora Schwartz!'

'Frau Schwartz!'

She stopped and turned round.

'I must ask a favour of you. Go to the chemist's, get me a bottle of . . . what is it called? A sedative. Any kind will do.'

'Mercy upon us! Don't you feel well?'

'I do not feel well. I pull the bell, but nobody answers. My man is out. I'm getting palpitations.'

Was he reduced to this, courtesy of the Kaiser, to telling fibs to a servant, depending on a servant? My God, they were certainly making him pay dear for the one little bit of enjoyment he tried to grab for himself.

La Schwartz headed downstairs, at top speed. The coast was clear.

The poor thing, his little bit of enjoyment, waiting so patient and obedient at her door. She listened to his excuses with anxiety and disappointment written all over her little face.

'Aren't you going to come in? Don't you want my music anymore?'

Music, what did music have to do with it? Did it have a double meaning? Was it a way of saying she was prepared for him to play her like an instrument, ready to surrender her love to him? No, impossible, she was too innocent.

'My dear, it will have to be another time. Something unexpected, something disagreeable, obligations. I was getting ready to come up here – in fact you must excuse the déshabille, quite unintended, I assure you – when in walks my Secretary and stays half an hour. And now I must see to things, set in motion, take steps.'

'I see. You're going to Wassen.'

'My love! Nothing of the kind, I've sent Gherardesca off to Wassen. I'd be glad to see the back of Wassen, I swear it. If only I could! I am all yours, yours alone. You know me, Clara . . .'

'Affairs of state?'

'That's it, affairs of state. Consider me a most unfortunate man, it's all I am. I leave you now, till this evening, till tomorrow. Tomorrow at five. You do understand, don't you? Until tomorrow then, here, at five, dead on.'

Scarcely was he back in his room when there came a loud knock on the door. Frau Schwartz, with Brighenti.

He grabbed the bottle.

'That's all I need. No. No! I'm better now, it's gone. Off you go, away with you now, both of you, and thank you. Thank you so very much.'

Clara did not put in an appearance at dinner. Frau Schwartz explained that the trouble was '*la migraine*'. Very sudden. Very strong.

Migraine, or a straight reprisal? Black as thunder Count Di Moriana stormed out to inspect her window from the road. It was tight shut, at only a quarter past eight. Windows speak their own language to men in certain states of mind, and he did not entertain the slightest doubt that he had understood this one. The girl felt slighted and was avenging herself upon him by having a tray brought up to her room, shutting herself away to punish him. And rightly so, since he had offended her in her innermost feminine dignity.

No matter that it was no fault of his, no matter that the one and only cause of his ruination was that pr–ck in his spiked helmet with the golden spread-eagle.

The devil take him, along with all his flunkeys and boot-lickers. And to think that he could be here in the morning, here in this little resort of Goeschenen, shattering the peace of it and wrecking everything, while he himself was compelled to welcome him, pay his respects and – the ultimate humiliation – embrace the odious creature.

Instead, next morning the thunder rolled away, as rapidly as it had come, as though by some wicked or comic spell.

'Next time really will be the last straw,' declared Gherardesca, who meantime had had the pleasure of his race at breakneck speed to Wassen and back in two hours flat, with a good stretch of it on the seat of his trousers. 'Yes, Brighenti,' he went on, raising his voice contrary to his usual mild nature, 'play one more trick on me like that and I swear I'll flatten that ugly goat-mug you were born with, and which the years haven't exactly im-proved.'

The Count, the one who was most affected, had taken it very calmly, Gherardesca later observed, like the good-hearted fellow he really was at bottom.

It went like this. At 6 a.m., in almost pitch darkness, Brighenti had come into his room to wake him. Gherardesca opened his eyes to find him actually sitting on the edge of his bed.

'I have an official announcement to make: he's not coming.'

'What's got into you, in heaven's name?'

Pushing back the sleeves of his nightshirt he ran to the wash-stand to bathe his face.

'So what is it?'

'*Al vèin megga.*'

'Eh?'

'Wilhelm. He's not coming.'

'Are you trying to make a fool of me?'

Brighenti busied himself throwing open the windows and shutters.

'Keep a window open at night. It stinks in here. It's one of the basic rules of hygiene, my friend. As for the Kaiser, before turning in last night I had another good look at his message. It's as plain as day. He was writing to say that he couldn't come.'

'Listen here, do you know German or don't you? Well?'

The Professor did not bat an eyelid.

'My dear chap, I've lived in Heidelberg, I've lived in Bonn, in Berlin. And what is more I've had various German girl-friends. Not that I wish to boast, I am a bachelor and I always was. And among them two Austrian girls, from Trieste. Always one at a time, mind you, apart from the two in Trieste. And in Berlin when I was a young fellow, as compliment to my bearing, my stature – no offence, old boy – my height of 181 centimetres, a girl I had used to call me her '*Gardeoffizier*'. *Adieu, mein kleiner Gardeoffizier*, ever heard the song? Well, no matter. Listen, I know German all right. But as a language it's on a par with Latin, nobody ever completely masters it. I suppose you've mastered Latin?'

'Go and get . . .'

'And an Emperor's style is difficult, it's elaborate, not like that of a stud-farmer. Pardon me, nothing personal, you know.'

But what was more to the point, who was going to break the news to the Count, this time round?

Gherardesca had 'no great desire'. 'I don't fancy it myself. Yesterday he took leave of his senses.'

'Ah but,' Brighenti retorted, 'as soon as I arrived on the scene he got a grip of himself. My presence was enough. *Praesente medico nihil nocet.* Still, it's true that he's a nervous type. Perhaps he ought to be spared some of his worries, the Secretariat might even intervene occasionally. To mitigate. To soften the blow.'

'Huh, listen to him! "The Secretariat." And what about the latest wrath of God, the one over the letter? Do you have the nerve to blame me?'

Brighenti straightened up to his full height. The champion of the people.

'Very well then, I shall take it upon myself to tell him. My conscience is clean. I fear not Kings, no tyrant makes me tremble. Adieu!'

But just to be on the safe side, he first sought out La Tschudi, the pretty teacher from Zürich, and presented for her inspection the knotty sentence, transcribed in the margin of an old copy of *Il Resto del Carlino*, his Bolognese daily paper. The authorised version (hers) exactly matched his own. So off he went to sit on a bench in front of the hotel in wordless colloquy with the immovable Wüntz, and to await the return of the Chief, who at that particular moment was witnessing a ceremony, one of the very few he was always glad to attend, on the rare occasions he was allowed the opportunity. In the yard of the little local school the children stood lined up two abreast, freckled and a little wooden and with their satchels on their backs, prior to receiving the order to troop into school. Schools and children, now those were two more things he liked.

Back home, at any rate in Monza, he would sometimes pay a visit to an elementary school, seating himself in a chair next to the teacher, under his own portrait and the map of Italy. (Francesco Crispi's Italy, each region painted a different colour, or every colour but red which cartographers were forbidden to use.) This sentimental attachment to childhood, a trait which for some reason seems to have escaped the royal anecdotists, was no pose and should not be too readily dismissed as a cliché. It was unwitting and instinctive, no less than his fatalistic indulgence towards his adversaries, including those who sought to bump him off and whom he would have rescued from the savagery of Italian justice, had it been in his power.

The little scholars filed into school, and he went back to the hotel.

Brighenti survived his ordeal unscathed. The Count's relief immediately expanded into gratitude, as though Wilhelm II advanced and retreated at the Professor's commands. The welcome surprise wiped out his resentment towards the man who had been responsible for the bad news, and a bad evening, and Brighenti was able to announce triumphantly:

'He stood me a coffee and a cigar, how about that! He is a great gentleman, the finest, but then I'm a man who's scared of nothing. By Jove, never grovel to anyone!'

Gherardesca still found it hard to believe.

'He calls me "my dear Brighenti", and then he says, do you know what he says? He says: In my House, you know, we have no talent for languages. We speak good French, pretty good Piedmontese, pretty bad Italian, and that's as far as it goes. The modesty of a great gentleman!'

A variety of spectacles was available to the village's summer visitors. There was the to-ing and fro-ing of the more dauntless among them, Anglo-Saxons for the most part, setting off to scale the glaciers with a tinkling arsenal of crampons, ice-picks and Alpenstocks, amid a picturesque retinue of guides and muleteers and porters, and as like as not returning with broken bones and half frozen to death. More frequent and enjoyable events were the arrivals of the St Gotthard diligence, its passengers alighting misshapen in shawls, scarves, veils, blankets, rucksacks and flasks (twice daily), and then the stops made by international trains (as many as four times a day). Not, perhaps, so widely appreciated were the long processions of cows winding their way through the village early in the morning and back again in the evening, between the byres and the nearer meadows. A boy would walk ahead of them, flapping a flag. The discordant clanging of the enormous cow-bells, some dangling right to the ground, had a dreamy solemnity about it, archaic, to the extent of causing one or two rare souls to experience a sudden nostalgia for snowy peaks and golden valleys: right there, when they were all around them. The dry resinous scent of pine and larch hanging on the air would be warmed for a moment by the animals' breath and the hay-smelling, fresh-steaming dung-pats dropping and splattering across the dust of the highway.

When they were off duty Brighenti and Gherardesca would divide their time between these various spectacles. That morning their Chief did not budge from the terrace of the Adler where two English girls were playing badminton, beating the 'shuttlecock' (in reality a small lump of lead with feathers stuck in it) to and fro, while he volunteered to umpire, without flinching when the cock smacked into him. Clara had appeared at a window, and the Count had managed to signal back: this afternoon, dead on five.

His two aides set off in the direction of the station to sample the first beer of the day. Outside the station a hulking brute of a man in sports clothes and a check cap with goggles strapped over the top was erecting a trestle. Then to the top of the trestle, or tripod, he screwed by continuous rotation, a square black leather box. At the appearance of a large cloth of the same colour people started to realise what was going on, and drew closer for a better look. A photographer. The man proceeded to appeal to the public in four languages: 1 franc the picture, success guaranteed, ready same day.

The two men, reconciled once more, exchanged amused and questioning looks. Then they stepped up, posed together arm in arm, and paid. 'Which hotel, gentlemen?' the photographer asked in Italian, and with an unmistakable Neapolitan accent. 'I'll deliver the result at five today.'

In the meantime an express had come and gone, and one or two passengers were emerging onto the square in front of the station.

'Hullo!' cried Brighenti. 'Isn't that Guillet over there?'

Yes, it was Guillet. Gherardesca's number two, looking lost and bewildered among the tourists, in frock coat and top hat, clutching an overcoat and attaché-case.

'What's the bad news?'

'What sun!' retorted Guillet, blinded by all those glaciers up there sparkling above the black canopy of pines. 'Someone get me a drink.'

They sat down at a secluded table in the Buffet. The former Guards officer, veteran of the 'last stand' at Villafranca, let them chatter on, telling their stories and asking questions, while he downed his beer in great gulps. Finally he took a newspaper out of his attaché-case and spread it before their eyes.

'There's the bad news.'

A well-known Rome newspaper, of very recent date. On the second page was an item across two columns, not long, but with an important caption, more sarcastic than enigmatic:

EUREKA!
WHERE CAN HE BE?
*From our own correspondent, in * * *, September*

Without addition or alteration there followed the 'story' filed that afternoon in the reading-room of the Adler by Walter Schiapin, alias Fairtales.

GHERARDESCA (*reading*): This *is* bad. Very. It's not going to be missed.

GUILLET: You thought no one would notice a thing, did you?

GHERARDESCA: Every precaution was taken.

GUILLET: When a prominent figure on his level ups and goes abroad it's always high life or high politics. The kind of thing journalists smell a thousand miles off.

GHERARDESCA: The Chief's no Saint Joseph but he avoids high society like the plague. And we're in a tiny village. In a little mountain hotel.

GUILLET: The article mentions a beautiful lady.

GHERARDESCA (*chuckles*): Don't jump to conclusions, Guillet, all it's about is a whole lot of money. We've sold the lady Visé, an old rats' nest near Monferrato in a bit of woodland. And at a pretty good price. A damn good price.

GUILLET: That may be true, but it's too simple to be believed. And this article is going to have repercussions. For instance, questions in the Chamber.

(*All are silent for a few seconds. A most pregnant pause.*)

GUILLET: Then there's Kaiser Wilhelm, remember. His presence has been reported in Romanshorn, on the Swiss side of Lake Constance. And that's a coincidence which no one is going to put down to pure chance. Everyone will assume a meeting is imminent.

BRIGHENTI (*proudly*): A meeting *was* immiment. And we two managed to avert it.

GUILLET: All the same, something is brewing, believe you me. Listen, precisely how much do you two gentlemen know about the Congo?

(GHERARDESCA *and* BRIGHENTI *eye each other with suspicion, until each is reassured by the silence of the other.*)

GUILLET: The Congo is a so-called independent state in Africa which has chosen to make Leopold King of the Belgians its sovereign. A country eighty-five times the size of Belgium and a mere five times as big as the German Empire. The Krupps, in the charity of their hearts, are of the opinion that it represents too grievous a burden for Leopold alone and so they have offered their assistance. Their proposal is a Belgian-German *Compagnie Minière*, with German capital and under German management. However, first they need to be sure that none of the European great powers, and in particular none in the Triple Alliance, will put a spoke in their wheel, to which end the Krupps have commissioned their good friend and ambassador, Wilhelm II, now happily enthroned, to sound out Vienna and Rome. Of course these are only rumours which are flying around, but *Le Figaro* is treating them extremely seriously, to the extent of dedicating an editorial to the question only last week.

GHERARDESCA: Krupp, you say? (*To* BRIGHENTI.) Our client, the beautiful lady in Wassen, is she not related to the Krupps?

BRIGHENTI (*worried*): I believe so.

GUILLET: Oh! Interesting.

GHERARDESCA: Let's get back to what concerns us, my dear Guillet. This article you've brought us, who put it together? Who can have tracked us down? A good many days we've been up here, and not one other Italian have we seen.

GUILLET: The question is naive. A journalist doesn't advertise his presence, he uses a disguise. You see that Monsignor over there in the corner drinking his *café-crème*? He could be a reporter for *Il Secolo*, or for the *Daily Mail*. The postilion, the mountain guide, the herdsman, the hotelier: any guise will do to conceal the journalist, the special correspondent. And up here in the middle of the mountains nothing would surprise me.

BRIGHENTI: Who would ever have thought it, eh? A nice little place like this, so peaceful and quiet – but, oh no, it's crawling with traitors, with spies.

GUILLET: But Switzerland, the whole of Switzerland, is the spies' paradise. Here you'll find undercover emissaries of the Sultan and of the Jesuits, spies for the Serbian Black Hand, agents of the Russian Okhrana and secret representatives of the Socialist International and the Anarchist International. Informers, conspirators, plotters, instigators of revolution and counter-revolution, not one of them is not represented, take my word for it.

GHERARDESCA (*slapping the table*): In heaven's name! The photographer! Five minutes ago. What if he's a reporter?

GUILLET: What photographer?

GHERARDESCA: He took our picture together, and now I come to think of it the station was right in the background. With that big sign saying 'Goeschenen, Uri.'

GUILLET: You two amaze me, in the Count's entourage and letting yourselves be photographed by someone you have never seen before!

GHERARDESCA: Good Lord! Brighenti, run and find him, I beg of you. Make him give you the photograph straightaway, whatever you have to do to get it.

BRIGHENTI (*rises to his feet, grim-faced, ready for the ultimate sacrifice*): So that's the way it is. Everything falls on my shoulders around here.

GUILLET: Professor, make him give you the plate as well. It's vital.

Brighenti hunted high and low through the village; he got dust in his hair and cow-dung on his shoes; he scoured every promenade and bridle-path and by-way up and down the banks of the Reuss. But the big man and his suitcase had vanished into thin air.

On his way back to the station, footsore and thirsty, he slipped into the *Bierstube*. To drink a *Bock*. On a hook in the cloak-room he spotted a check cap.

'Yes,' confirmed the landlord, who by now looked upon Brighenti as a regular customer. 'The photographer is upstairs.

He asked for a room where he could print his pictures, and I gave him one.'

That settled it, the man had to be a spy. Otherwise he'd still be out there taking pictures. Theirs was the only one he wanted, obviously. Brighenti had no hesitation. He was Bolognese, he had guts, upstairs he went, rapped on a door and stuck his head inside.

'Shut it! This is a dark-room. *Machen Sie die Tür zu!*'

'I'll stand for no nonsense, young man. I am the person in the picture you took in front of the station. And I want the plate as well.'

'You're ruining the lot! Are you out of your mind? Shut the bleeding door!'

'You'll be lucky. You just give me what you'd better give me.'

The man sprang out of the dark, pushed the photograph into his hand, still wet, and slammed the door. Brighenti flung it open again.

'I demand that plate. And be warned, you can't take me for a ride. You'll not get away with this. Nobody can fool . . .'

Before he reached the end of his speech he was flying across the landing.

'Bugger off, you old bastard! See them stairs? Get down them or I'll boot you down!'

The man had the strength of an ox.

Brighenti, picking up the photograph, descended the stairs. Without waiting for further encouragement, but with dignity, and on his own two legs.

By the time he got back to his companions his mission had taken him more than an hour and Guillet was already on his way. On the eleven o'clock train for Italy. Gherardesca explained:

'Guillet only came here to draw my attention to the article and put me in the picture. Any decisions will rest with me.'

And seeing the photograph:

'Bless me, it's a work of art. That's the living likeness of the two of us. And there's the sign right behind. "Goeschenen, Uri", just as I thought. So what about the plate?'

'I smashed it over his head.'

As had indeed been his intention, and Brighenti was no Jesuit to go making fine distinctions between the act and the intent.

Back at the hotel they sought out the Count and made cautious inquiries. Yes, a photographer had indeed appeared, he had come out onto the terrace. The Count, naturally, had sent him packing. But nicely, with two francs in his hand.

'Do you expect me to let people take pictures? We're in much too delicate a position to be dreaming of taking any souvenirs back. And you two? I don't suppose it crossed either of your minds to . . .?'

As one man:

'Signor Conte, the very thought!'

A joint lie, hence self-confessed. But if the intention is good?

The bell had not yet sounded for luncheon, and there was time for them to repair to one of their bedrooms. To confer. The Professor inclined to the view that it would be best to say nothing, either about the news item or Guillet's appearance.

'That's easy for you to say. But for me it's another matter, I have certain responsibilities to face.'

'Well, I can face mine. I'll sign a medical bulletin declaring I prescribed a fortnight's total rest. What's wrong with doing that? He's been taking a well-earned break from his duties. And he left word where he would be, or how else could Guillet have found us? No one can say he is untraceable.'

'But he is, officially. That's why we can't let this thing get out. And that's not the end of it. There's this blessed coincidence of the Emperor's presence in the same corner of Europe. They'll be saying that they have seen each other.'

'Issue an official denial.'

In the end the proposal to say nothing prevailed. On their return to Monza Gherardesca would slip the news cutting into the file marked 'In hand'. The Chief would get to read it by and by, but long enough after the event. Brighenti still had worries about those German intrigues in the Congo.

'Ever since '71,' observed Gherardesca, 'that's for the past eighteen years, we've been hearing much more worrying news. Every spring there's talk of a French *revanche* for their defeat and of a pre-emptive strike by Prussia. Storm clouds that soon blow over. But far be it from me to pass judgment, it's politics and politics is not my business.'

Brighenti sniggered.

'And when I think there are people at Court who call you the Florentine Secretary. Some Machiavelli you make!'

'I am a Tuscan, not a Florentine, and I'll have you know I'm not that kind of secretary. Pay less heed to the silly things people say. I've heard it said some people even call you Aesculapius.'

But this whole affair of the newspaper article was something which they couldn't so easily banish from their minds, or simply dismiss with a couple of gibes. A journalist who arrives all the way from Rome at just the right moment: someone must have tipped him off. And having reached the place, in whatever disguise, wherever he had hidden out, he must still have needed instructions or information, a precise trail to follow. The article even mentioned Frau Von Goltz. It described Frau Von Goltz's chalet in Wassen, it alluded to meetings between the Count and the lady.

There is a Judas in our midst.

The two men looked sidelong at each other. Compelled by virtue of their respective posts to be always together, united by a mutual antipathy, party for the past half hour to the same (necessary) lie, inseparable and firmly convinced they were the fiercest adversaries.

'A Judas . . .' Gherardesca said, echoing his own thoughts aloud. 'And when I find him I'll break his face.'

'Fiddlesticks. Anyway, how are you going to find him?'

'I'll break his face for him, I will. And there'd better be no chance it's yours.'

'Mine? When you spend all day sharing little secrets with Frau Tschudi . . .'

'Yours, I said. Seeing how you can never keep off – to coin a phrase – Frau Schwartz.'

'Are you daring to . . .'

'Not yet. I reserve the right to dare.'

'Then are you ready to challenge me to a duel, Count?'

'Right now, Professor, I challenge you to luncheon.'

The Professor, having already faced so many challenges that morning, had worked up quite an appetite.

'I accept.'

X

————————•————————

The first fortnight of September 1889: remembered in the annals of the city not for any notable deeds or extraordinary or exemplary achievements, but for the heat. Ferocious. It was reliably calculated that of more than four hundred thousand souls ('Rome is getting to be a real metropolis') no more than two hundred thousand remained, veritable souls in torment, the rest having fled to seek salvation on the beaches and hills of Latium. The Tiber, no more than a yellow trickle between rusty cans of corned beef and old calcium-encrusted chamberpots. The renowned aqueducts barely dribbling. In the *Campagna* the earth cracked open before people's eyes, as if they were witnessing an earthquake.

The Prefect of the Capital had a nasty accident. Sole surviving incarnation of Order, all the civic authorities having quit the scene, not to mention Government and Parliament in hiding since weeks before, the good functionary considered himself duty bound to stand in for them as best he could by conducting daily rounds of inspection within and without the Walls. One evening he went out along the Via Laurentina and on his way back his horses suddenly shied, and not without good cause, sending the carriage into a tree and the Prefect and his escort to hospital. Three or four buffaloes had surged out of the bushes onto the road, horns lowered. Driven by thirst they had come all the way from the Pontine Marshes which the great drought had almost succeeded in draining, something not even the Popes had ever managed to achieve.

Similar items of news, together with the meteorological reports and gloomy forecasts, filled the papers and supplied the needs of their sweltering readers, all other news palling in comparison. The two half-columns by WS, those 'intimate revelations' from ***, did not arouse the response they deserved or reach the particular readership they were designed for: politicians, diplomats, socialites. They were totally wasted, like lighting a Roman candle under the midday sun. Under *that* sun.

Nevertheless from the Baths of Bognanco one top politician did send a dispatch to another top politician drinking the waters at the Springs of Fiuggi. The dispatch was *en claire*, i.e. not in code, and hence far from clear. With judicious imprecision it alluded to the remarkable journalistic revelation regarding a certain 'well-known figure' and requested the views of the recipient with 'full details' of the course of action he proposed to adopt. Fiuggi's reply was curt and caustic, requesting fuller details of the details requested. Bognanco pressed again, repeating well-nigh without variation the text of the first telegram which, so it appeared, was deemed to be entirely comprehensible if not, for obvious reasons, perfectly explicit.

The truth is that these two correspondents, the one in Fiuggi and the one in Bognanco, had no love for each other (the very opposite), and even less respect. As happens in such cases, it was already hard enough for them to understand each other orally. So what other outcome could there be?

Fiuggi failed to take any action or even reply. The article had been read and noted, but whether or not the well-known figure was on a spree in German Switzerland, or for that matter the Austrian Tyrol, when he should have been in Salice d'Ulzio, was not considered to be the point at issue. Quite the contrary. A number of reports indicated that also present in German Switzerland during those same days was a far more active and significant figure. None other than the supreme representative of the dominant axis of power — Germany, Prussia, Berlin — round which our country's foreign policy needed increasingly to revolve. If the Two had had a meeting then it would have been no bad thing. As far as one of the Two was concerned, quite possibly the first good idea that had ever occurred to him.

That Roman candle fizzling in the midday sun, only just detected in Bognanco and Fiuggi, was picked up from as far away as Bern. The Foreign Department of the Swiss Confederation, though less directly concerned in this specific instance, possessed extremely sensitive antennae. And a most meticulous sense of courtesy. And curiosity.

The Chief of Protocol was instructed to proceed to Canton Uri and look into the matter. This explains why a gentleman of neutral aspect with the manners of a notary, alighted from the train at Goeschenen and having completed swift inquiries at the Hotel Adler installed himself in the Des Alpes.

His mission was accomplished in a very few hours. That same morning, having positioned himself behind a newspaper at a table on the terrace of the Adler where he had ordered coffee and *petit-pains*, and having watched a game of shuttlecock in the company of a stout, bewhiskered Italian of ripe years (who amused himself by playing umpire for the girls in the game), he convinced himself that there could be no doubts in the matter. Retiring from the scene, he presently returned and asked to speak to Count Di Moriana's Secretary.

At that hour (2 p.m.) the porter was absent at lunch, and the man who answered his inquiry was the hotel proprietor. 'Answered' is an exaggeration: Wüntz looked over his shoulder, jerked a thumb at Brighenti who was sitting in an easy-chair in the lobby, and then resumed the contemplative attitude of Buddha-hotelier, arms folded behind his back, against the front door-post.

'I have an announcement,' said the visitor, 'for the Count.'

Brighenti sprang to his feet.

'Stop right there! Who are you?'

The man introduced himself.

'Oh no, you don't. You people are not going to catch me out again. You're a newspaper man.'

'I am not a newspaperman.'

'In that case you're a photographer.'

'Neither am I a photographer,' replied the other man, with a smile of deep understanding.

'And how come you speak better Italian than I do? When you say you are from Bern?'

'I come from Ticino, from Stabio. But that does not make me any the less Swiss and capable of being attached to a particular Department, as I explained to you. Or Ministry, as you say in your country.'

'Then show me your credentials.'

'You shall see them at once. Just give me the time to go back to my hotel.'

'Where?'

'Hotel Des Alpes.'

'I'm coming with you.'

The credentials were duly produced, and Brighenti had to change his tone.

'Well, Councillor?'

'Well, Professor, it is my duty to report to you that the Federal Government is cognizant of the honour which the Count has bestowed upon us in electing to sojourn in one of our Cantons. And it places itself entirely at his disposal to attend to his every need for as long as he remains on Swiss territory.'

'I shall be honoured to pass that on.'

'The Federal Government will take every step to ensure that the Count's peace is in no way disturbed. Furthermore, it deeply regrets the deplorable incident resulting from an excess of zeal on the part of our frontier guards.'

'Frontier guards? Incident? And when was all this?'

'Some days ago.'

'Nobody told me about it.'

'No matter, Professor. For further eventual travel within our borders, or to effect his return to his own country, the Count Di Moriana, should he so wish, is at liberty to make use of a special *wagon-salon* of the Federal Railways. From tomorrow morning it will be waiting for him, at Goeschenen station.'

'How very kind. You have assured me that your Government wishes to respect the peace of its illustrious guest. May I therefore inquire for what reason it has decided to intervene? Might it be in response to indiscretions appearing in the Italian press?'

It was a little ingenuous of the Professor to expect a Chief of Protocol to unbosom himself with him.

'No important items of news which appear in the foreign press are overlooked by the Department of Foreign Affairs.'

And that was that.

While retracing his steps to the Adler Brighenti ran into Gherardesca, right on the bridge over the Reuss.

'Naturally an incorrigible idler like yourself has never got round to taking a look at the river before.'

Brighenti was in no mood for joking.

'On the contrary, after what I've been through these past two days I'd be prepared to go back to Porretta for good and all. I am a doctor. Not a Talleyrand!'

Together they leaned over the bridge, and he gave a full report of the visit of the man from Bern.

'Well, so what are your thoughts on the subject?'

'Easy. Our incognito is a farce. It has more holes than a sieve.'

'So what should we do? Are we going to tell him?'

'We could. But if we do that he is going to want to know how the people in Bern ever got to hear of it. And then we'll have to say it was in an Italian newspaper. "And the newspaper, how did a paper get to hear of it?" And so we are back to square one: who betrayed our secret? I don't know where this is going to end, because one thing is for sure, there are only three of us who can possibly be suspected, if we really have to include Vigliotti as well.'

There was, to be quite accurate, also La Goltz. But both quickly agreed that the lady was the least likely suspect. She wouldn't have dealings with Italian hack reporters, as Brighenti phrased it.

They lapsed into silence, watching the green waters of the Reuss flowing beneath them.

'And that accursed Department for Foreign Affairs,' Brighenti resumed after a while, with sincere bitterness, 'which goes and puts its illustrious guest under special surveillance. Not having the guts to say: you must notify us of all your movements and of when you decide to leave Switzerland – they dream up their little ruse about a saloon wagon. Cunning as foxes!'

'And so we come back to the fact of Wilhelm's presence here as well. The Swiss are very jealous of their neutrality.'

A rumble of wheels was heard, the sound of hooves beating fast, and then the Gotthard mail-coach on its way down from the pass swept past their backs, almost touching them.

'My dear chap, so long as there were only carriages,' went on Gherardesca slapping the dust off his clothes as it continued to settle on him, 'a sovereign's incognito had a fair chance of surviving. But not now, not with all these new-fangled means of communication concocted by modern technology. Railways, the telegraph. Things which, mind you, can make smuggling a bit of an easier proposition. That incident with the frontier guards, don't you know what he was referring to?'

'I don't.'

'"I don't." Shocking memory you have. When we came back from Monza, that morning. You had a crate of twenty-four bottles of San Giovese, did you not? Or was it Albano? And you sat there quiet as a mouse, didn't you, so you wouldn't have to pay duty. Have you forgotten how the Swiss customs officer at the frontier spotted it and told you to open it? Come on, own up.'

'I have not forgotten. Because they were intended for my own consumption I didn't know you had to pay duty.'

'What a brain. And the result is the "deplorable incident".'

'I did it in good faith, and you know it!'

'All I know is that you are about to go down in the diplomatic history of the nineteenth century. Because now you are going to write to Bern with a full explanation. And you'll sign it too, name and surname, for all to see.'

'What's got into your head?'

'Ah, you'll not get off this time. Do you intend to cast a permanent shadow over relations between the Swiss Confederation and the Savoy Monarchy? Do you suppose for the sake of twenty-four bottles of wine, however drinkable, I'd let you do a thing like that?'

Impatient, trembling, equipped (he reckoned) with sufficient amorous appeal, rash to the point of having at the last moment exchanged his jacket and waistcoat for a dressing-gown (silk, with a big floral design) he scaled the stairs and traversed the corridors (empty, empty!) towards his rendezvous. At 17.00 hours (less a minute or two) he knocked on that bedroom door.

The door, in fact, was ajar. He stepped inside.

And at that very moment the pretty maid burst into tears. Sitting on the edge of her bed, in a rose and sky-blue negligée, with a face that was damp, dashed, desolate, and very determined.

In the long instants which followed the Count's feelings had time to pass from surprise to irritation, from irritation to fury, and finally to pity. He held her hand. He squeezed it with genuine concern. But, after a little while, he had to put it back on the pillow.

'But I'm not here to hurt you! What is it?'

Clara sobbed.

'No, no, don't do that! Please don't. I have no intention of forcing myself upon you.'

'Oh, poor me!'

'If it is your virtue that you fear for, I promise you I prize it very highly.'

'My virtue? Hah!'

'Well then?'

'My virtue, today is . . . it's in no danger. Since yesterday, as a matter of fact.'

Now he began to understand.

'The migraine?'

Through the tears peeped a little smile, which quickly broadened and exploded into a burst of laughter. Piercing. Then:

'*C'est l'homme qui propose, c'est Dieu qui indispose* . . . But, Count, it's so embarrassing.'

Floods of tears again. The Count thumped his forehead.

'Well, isn't that just my luck! Anyway,' he concluded, 'you mustn't cry anymore. That's enough now. We shall just have to resign ourselves.'

'How good you are to me. If only you knew how fond of you I am already. Pardon me, I should say: how devoted I am.'

'Sweet child. Here, upon my chest.'

An embrace. Returned in anything but timid fashion.

'But how can I? You're not a man. You are Italy. The flag. How could I ever?'

'Don't say such things!' – suddenly he shot to his feet – 'I am a man!'

The situation bordered on the ideal, and on the other hand it was perilously approaching the comic. Even he perceived it and reached for the doorhandle, to be gone.

'Don't leave me, Count, I beg you. If I think I may never see you again . . .'

'Stand up, and come out into the corridor, it's less risky. Now we can talk.'

Meekly she followed him out, and they talked. First he reassured her. 'We shall see each other again, very often, because I have something in mind. Vigliotti is one of the best aides on my staff and I am proposing to give him a job that will keep him by me, in my household. He is an officer, but he is entitled to ask to be put on reserve.'

'Next month,' Clara reminded him earnestly, 'we are getting married.'

'He'll have his full leave entitlement. And as for a wedding present, I leave the suggestion to you.'

In her openness the 'child' made no attempt to conceal the fact that she had expected a present. She and Vigliotti were both of them very well-off but unfortunately Vigliotti, though of course 'most gentlemanly', was not a gentleman by birth, being nothing more than 'Signor' Vigliotti, a condition which was humiliating to him, both in her presence and in Court society. Might it not be possible to help him over his little inhibitions, reward him somehow?

The Count immediately concluded that the one to feel humiliated was not so much Vigliotti as his fiancée. And he did not approve. Swelling the limitless list of the Italian nobility had never been a thing he favoured; in a world, moreover, which was already securely in the hands of the barons of commerce and the captains of industry.

To promote him straightaway, prior to going on reserve, would be the thing to do; in fact it had occurred to him before and it was perfectly acceptable. And so for the second time (less

Platonically than the first) he clasped the child to his bosom and then fled the scene. Reassuring, tiptoeing, smiling, ambiguous.

'You will be satisfied, never fear, I promise you. And now we must leave each other, but only for an hour. Only one hour!'

The smile suddenly faded from his lips: standing in the corridor outside his room was Gherardesca, with a very long face.

He had come to ask the Chief about his plans for the immediate future. It did not promise to be an easy task, dressing up in artful circumlocutions the one question which could be postponed no longer: did he intend returning home, or not? If not, a whole series of provisions would need to be made, instructions for Monza, announcements for Rome. There were also one or two difficulties of a simple logistic nature. (Within a few days the hotel was due to close, as it did at the end of every season.)

There was no need for his circumlocutions, or even his question. For a long time the Chief had not picked up a newspaper or looked at a calendar, and yet with every nerve in his body he felt time passing. In a way he had never felt it before, so remorselessly fast and elusive, and for the simple reason that it would have been wonderful to be able to slow it down, and hold it.

That morning after getting up he had taken out his note-book.

Against the 6th September was written: *Remember to go back home*. Underlined twice, and with a large arrow in the margin so that he would not overlook it.

Two days later: 'No one has bothered me, either from Rome or Monza. I have forgotten them and they have forgotten me. Wüntz (the proprietor of the Adler) has the same function here that I have at home, except that he is more decorative. And yet I must go back, my resignation was only temporary.'

10th September: *Watch out for the passage d'âge when back home*. Underlined twice.

'I agree, Gherardesca. You are right, we must go back. You do all the preparations, the arrangements, the announcements and so forth. And then half an hour, one hour, before departure come to me and say: We're off. You decide the day, you decide the moment. Understood?'

'Perfectly. Everything will be done as you say.'

'Right up to the last moment I want to know nothing. *Politique de l'autriche*, am I right?'

'I don't know. I don't think so.'

'And pity me too, if you like, I should not take it amiss.'

Just one question. Did he wish, before leaving, to send a token of his appreciation, a little gift of some kind, to Frau Von Goltz? Vigliotti could be sent to purchase something, in Altdorf or Lucerne. Some flowers perhaps?

'Not enough.'

'A bracelet?'

'Too intimate.'

'Might a flower-bowl be the thing, in silver, engraved with the donor's initials and the royal crown?'

'M'm, that might do. Agreed.'

His timing as perfect as ever, on hand at the mere mention of his name, Vigliotti was at that very instant arriving. They heard the sound of gravel crunching under the wheels of a carriage as it swung into the drive and came to a halt; they heard Vigliotti's voice, and then a few words in German uttered by a woman who made even those gutturals and aspirates a pleasure to hear.

La Goltz. Gherardesca was dispatched downstairs at once.

In Hungary – he mused to himself as he gazed down from the window – they have hit on an ideal solution to the problem. When Count Czernin is in the countryside, where it looks so out of keeping to go round with servants in livery and top hats, his coachmen and footmen are dressed like huntsmen. Somewhere between huntsmen and hussars. Soft boots, dark green tunic with black braiding down the front, bowler hat with a Tyrolean-style plume in it. Here in the mountains La Goltz adopts the same model for her equipage. Now we couldn't do that in Monza, because Monza is a copy of the Quirinal. In summer the Duke of Norfolk inspects his farms accompanied by lackeys in livery. Ah yes, but not for nothing has Norfolk remained a Catholic, he's one for pomp and display. The Hungarian model – Czernin's, Esterhazy's – now I find that most apt, while still sufficiently fanciful. More modern, almost. Yet in their country it's the custom. A very old one, too, who knows how old.

Gherardesca interrupted his reflections.

'I have shown the lady up to the first-floor sitting-room.'

'I'm on my way.'

The lady's costume was fashion-plate Paris. A pity he was only half aware of it, in no position to appreciate it properly, but women's fashion was not his forte. On the other hand he was struck, yet again, by the Parisian quality of La Goltz's French: remarkable. She excused herself for calling unannounced. She had wanted to bid him goodbye before her own departure and also assure him that the matter of the mortgage had been satisfactorily settled.

'Vigliotti has managed to convince both myself and Herr Grüber. In Signor Vigliotti the Count has a most able representative.'

'So I have seen,' he said, without meaning the remark to be pointed. He was in the best possible mood, considering the circumstances.

'We are prepared to assume fifty per cent of the cost of redemption. Perhaps, in exchange, you would be so kind as to do me a favour.'

'At your service.'

Well now. She had plans for Visé, she would be visiting the estate regularly and intended transforming all the land under cultivation into vineyards where she would be introducing *Moselwein* vine-stock. It would be necessary to purchase machinery and recruit local labour, and to that end she needed someone of ability with a good knowledge of the area, and it was her hope that Vigliotti would be able to superintend operations, get things underway. Oh, it would be quite enough for him to come over once or twice a month, his duties permitting, naturally, and with his Master's gracious approval. Which she most warmly solicited.

Indefinable as always was the colour of those eyes, and as distinguished as ever, very superior, was her entire person, and yet to him she seemed to have aged a little. No, not aged: faded. The bloom, the radiance had left her. It was as though a film of dust had settled on her face, her neck, even her hands.

This time, he thought, the advantage is mine. He experienced the sweetness of revenge, subtle and exhilarating. Highly agreeable.

The little group of attendants waiting outside was admitted into the room; Grüber for La Goltz, Vigliotti and Gherardesca. Vermouth and conversation followed, and since it was soon past seven o'clock he had little option but to invite her to join them for dinner.

The Count's table accommodated La Goltz, Vigliotti, and Clara. He himself, though formally the senior member of the little party, was little more than a spectator for much of the time. To take his mind off La Goltz's nervous persistent chatter he began to observe the engaged couple. Vigliotti was not loquacious (he never was) or ingratiating; he avoided addressing Clara directly and made no attempt to encourage her to concern herself with him. And yet he was most scrupulous in looking after her needs and attentive to what she said, readily let her speak for him, accompanying her replies with little nods of approval in a display of conjugal solidarity that was exemplary, already masterly. Precisely what happens when two well-bred spouses have learned to replace decayed love with good manners and mutual respect.

Between Vigliotti and La Goltz: nothing. They ignored each other. La Goltz badgered Clara remorselessly, beginning by addressing her as 'Signorina' and calling her '*mon amie*' and '*ma petite*' by the end. She quizzed her with tact and without any hint of irony, sympathetically and methodically, much as a conscientious and well-meaning teacher with no illusions about having to fail a candidate will multiply questions and kindnesses in order to sweeten the inevitable outcome.

The poor girl stood up to it as best she could. At first she put on a 'little kitten' air, later she sought to deflect fire towards Vigliotti and even in his own direction ('Perhaps the Count can answer that better than I can') and to wriggle off the hook ('In Italy you have no idea how badly girls are taught'). In the end she gave unmistakable signs of fatigue, playing for time by resorting to giggles which she was careful not to allow to degenerate into squeals ('What terrible French I'm speaking!') and defending herself with smiles which were less and less convincing and more and more forced. When she was on the brink of having to give her, most reluctantly, thumbs down, La Goltz abruptly broke off the interrogation and turning away from the girl addressed to the most important diner some non-committal remarks concerning hunting in the mountains (the need to protect Alpine fauna from hunters who are too clever). And then, without any further beating about the bush:

'Our engaged couple' – stressing that possessive adjective – 'are travelling round Europe in a few weeks' time, Count.'

'Europe?'

'For their honeymoon, of course. And do you know what I am going to do? I shall prepare a nice little nest for them – oh, only a temporary one, naturally! – at Bad Gastein, on the Rhine, where I always spend the autumn. My house in Bad Gastein happens to contain a little apartment which seems just made for them.'

'Our' couple? What did she mean by it? Why, did they each have a share in them, was the couple on detachment to himself and La Goltz?

In effect, it was perfectly true. Before her arrival an hour ago La Goltz had known nothing, and now she was fully in the picture, already she understood everything: women are like that. But such arrogance was not something he went along with. Her way of harping on the point, the tiny hints, all her false tact. No, he wasn't going to allow it. It crossed his mind that Francesco Mèlito (the Duke Di Mèlito Portosalvo, a close friend) went cruising in his yacht every October.

'Vigliotti, I'll find the two of you a couple of cabins on board Francesco Mèlito's big boat. You're a sailor, you'll be more than welcome. You'll have your honeymoon at sea.'

Vigliotti and consort thanked him.

'There's only one thing to remember. Mèlito hates being called Excellency. Just call him Don Cicce.'

As September progresses, with the increasingly oblique angle of the sun at its rising, the peaks and glaciers seen from the Adler can look very close on clear mornings, almost as though you could stroke them, and at the same time as remote as dreams, or memories. Already on the terrace by seven o'clock, he noticed this too; he even looked at them for a moment, a fairly long moment, until Mancuso arrived with his coffee and all the trimmings. A window opened, and the lathered cheeks of Professor Brighenti appeared and disappeared.

By a miracle of speed, Brighenti was down on the terrace at 7.15 to bid good morning to his employer and to ask his permission to be allowed to put forward an 'idea'. He was careful to emphasise that he was speaking in his capacity of personal physician.

'Am I correct in thinking that in spite of that accident the Count does not retain a disagreeable impression of the stage-coach? I refer to the St Gotthard diligence.'

'And why should I, pray?'

'Very good. Yet I seem to remember that on the way here the train gave you some trouble, the small compartment, all that smoke in the tunnels. Anyway, just in case, I made a few inquiries and I understand that the diligence does a weekly run between Goeschenen and Como, by way of Bellinzona and Lugano.'

'Oh yes? And who uses it?'

'Foreigners. English, Germans . . .'

There followed a digression (the Count kept eating steadily) on the beauty of escaping from the frenetic tempo of modern life, particularly as embodied in its all-consuming technology, such as the telegraph (and soon we shall have the telephone), electric lighting, the giddy speed of the railway train. The man of today feels a need to take a step back, all the more so if he belongs to one of those nations where progress is rampant, a little step backwards into the past, back to natural horse-power, to roads without rails. To the old diligences, the stage-coaches, of our youth.

'Or rather, let me hasten to correct myself, of my youth.'

'And so?'

Having reached the heart of the matter, Brighenti faltered a moment.

'Well, Count. What I did was I went and asked at the post-station whether they might be able, whether it would be at all possible should the need arise, to provide a coach, a reserved carriage, for the route I just mentioned. From here to Como takes between ten and eleven hours, including halts. Were a telegram to be sent, the Palace could dispatch carriages to Como, which would be waiting there to convey us to Monza.'

The Count spread butter and honey on the freshly baked rolls – exquisite. That *Bäckerei*, what skill. That baker-woman, the one with the geraniums.

Brighenti had thought of everything. The baggage could go by train, and Gherardesca as well, seeing he preferred the train. Vigliotti would follow on later, since he was to go on a shopping expedition to Lucerne. That meant there would be three of them: the Count, Brighenti himself, and Mancuso. However Brighenti had a further proposal to make, the most delicate of all. Whether it was due to his cunning or sheer good luck, the Count's little court in Goeschenen was still unaware of his 'flirtation' with Clara Mansolin; and here Brighenti gave the lie to the common belief that doctors, in this particular area of human behaviour, are good observers.

He cleared his throat.

'I hope you will forgive me, Count, if I have presumed to take an unpardonable liberty. I happen to have mentioned my idea, with all due discretion of course, to Signorina Mansolin and to Frau Schwartz. They declared themselves honoured, but I left things in the air. Pending, need I say, or rather subject to, your approval. Attach no weight, Count, to this private suggestion of mine. Which places no one under any obligation, not even myself.'

The Count raised his head at last:

'And what if I should say that the Gotthard coach gains my full approval?'

A moment or two later Brighenti withdrew, with two successes to his credit: the fact of having convinced the Chief to take up an idea of his ('Never grovel to anyone!' 'Who is this man anyway, a despot, a medieval monarch, or just a man like me?'); secondly, for the return journey to have substituted two nice females for that confounded stuck-up Florentine (Gherardesca) who seemed to think he was at liberty to ridicule and maltreat his fellow-man, for God alone knows what reason. (Perhaps because he supposed himself to be descended from a cannibal?) And add to that the satisfaction of hoodwinking the Chief of Protocol in Bern. Aye, foiling the foxy Swiss.

After the Professor's departure, the Count lit up a cigar and turned his chair to face the mountains ('Magnificent, magnificent'). He took out his watch, and saw it was half past seven. He still had an entire morning ahead of him, then, to be enjoyed.

'And then – *finita la libertà finita la festa* – when freedom is over the party's over. I become myself again. I go back into my own skin.'

Gherardesca (whose own learning extended little further than horses) was wont to say of his Chief: 'Uncultivated? Not specially, only a little. Ignorant? Why, no more than necessary.'

Candid, of that there is no doubt. In that century which discovered the *ego*, if someone had said to him: freedom means no more than the liberty to be *myself* and be able to live in my own skin, he would have been staggered. Even indignant, probably.

In any case, he had a few hours left to himself. And are not a few hours a bit of life? He would go for a walk on his own, one more time, stop when he liked, look at whatever he wanted to. Spit out the stub of his cigar and scratch himself between the shoulder-blades whenever he felt like it.

He would go as far as the kiosk along the Larchwood Promenade. And on his way back he would have another look at the houses in the village, one by one, right to where the road to Wassen begins. He knew – this at least he knew for certain – that he would never see them again, and he wanted to look at all of them one last time. He could also, on some pretext or other, pop into the *Bäckerei* and take a closer look, finally, at the big girl with the geraniums.

He got up, in a hurry now, and crossed the hall. Mancuso was close on his heels with his stick and his hat which he had forgotten on the terrace.

At his exit Herr Wüntz moved aside just enough to let him pass and answered the cordial wave of his hand (he never greeted anyone first) before resuming his position against the door-post.

AFTERWORD

————————•————————

Dear Madam Reader, The story which you are about to put down, as archaic and ingenuous as my appealing to you, means to imply no more than it says. Plausible yet tenuous, it confines itself to its flower-stands and mantelpieces, its coaches and steam-engines – a world of vanished things which seem almost incredible now, and which nonetheless have been, for me, an essential theme, anything but decoration. A simple story with no special significance, and with nothing to teach, since it is far too well known that there is no life, no matter how inauspicious or ill-fated, in which comedy has no part to play.

And now, reading back over it, the comedy makes me think of Meilhac and Halévy. Without, I fear, Offenbach's champagne-like music. Of Daudet too, but without the epic quality of his *Tartarin* and its proto-ecological polemic. In any case there is no question that these pages are uncommitted and demand no commitment from you. They hark back to a remote Italy and to one of its personalities who, though officially the hero of the tale in every way, is really no more than a pretext. Today he is neither celebrated nor denigrated. To tell the truth, he is not even remembered.

A flight from reality among the phantoms of the Belle Epoque? I would not deny it. Neither do I offer any excuses. I do not hold that a book need necessarily be escapist, even if its subject is escape. (From a job, in this case, which was among the most loathsome and alienating – and to which most reacted as a rule with an extreme fatuity.) No, this is a little book which exploits and delights in escape, quite intentionally. And therefore openly. It parades its most gratuitous and hare-brained features.

I am also perfectly ready to accept the notion, itself a cliché by now, that the Belle Epoque never existed. The most I would say is that we still have need of fables, and that that particular myth is as good as another. Like its own specific language, which I have sought to imitate.

Lastly, dear Madam, take this little tale in the spirit of its title. One person at least, I who wrote it, was diverted.

GM